S–L–O–W
Dancer

A CONNIE KALE INVESTIGATION

Books by Rodman Philbrick

Slow Dancer
Brothers and Sinners

J.D. Hawkins Mystery Series
Shadow Kills
Ice for the Eskimo
Paint it Black
Walk On the Water

T.D. Stash Mystery Series
The Neon Flamingo
The Crystal Blue Persuasion
Tough Enough

S–L–O–W
<u>Dancer</u>

W. R. Philbrick

SPEAKING VOLUMES, LLC

NAPLES, FLORIDA

2012

Slow Dancer

ISBN 978-1-61232-837-9

For my brothers, Philip, Jonathan, and Mark

Chapter One

He called himself The Man of Steel, which has a certain poignancy in light of what happened later, after he'd finished the business of taking his clothes off and he and Mandy O'Hare walked down Front Street to the Sea Breeze Motel, holding hands in the moonlight like a couple of kids, one of them thinking about love and the other getting ready to die.

The murder occurred at around four in the morning, but I didn't hear about it until a little after twelve noon, when I went downtown to take my medicine at Shorty's Downeast Cafe. The "downeast" is a concession to the tourists who straggle through this harbor town in season. What matters to a native like me is that the coffee is strong and clear.

I'd been out to the homestead the night before, where I'd mixed big drinks and small conversation with my father. As a result it was difficult to focus on the headlines in the *Rivermuth Record,* which someone had left on the counter. It was Shorty who put his big thumb on the captioned pho-

I

tograph and asked me wasn't it true I used to be a friend of the deceased.

It was true enough, once upon a time. But the truth didn't immediately penetrate through the dull ache in my forehead. That was my father's fault. He was the one who wheeled himself over to the cupboard and produced the sealed bottle of Irish whiskey. Heavy drinking doesn't run in the family; nevertheless we managed to ruin the bottle, and all the while the old man sat there looking mean enough to bite the head off a rabid bat.

The silence was as sturdy as a fieldstone wall between us. I knew he wanted to tell me again what a fool I'd been to quit the tour and give up the career we'd both planned for me. It was no good telling him I'd quit because I wasn't good enough. He wouldn't believe a word of it. He still insists I have the best swing he's ever seen on a woman and that I ought to use it somehow, if not on the tour, then as a club pro, teaching and making the local rounds.

I won't bother going into what my old man thinks about my present career. Suffice to say he has chosen to ignore it altogether, which tends to stifle our conversations almost as much as the fact that he can no longer speak.

Don't get the idea I don't love the old guy. It's just that being Johnny Kale's daughter has its complications. The truth is I regret blowing my chance almost as much as he regrets blowing his. Maybe it would have been easier for us both if my mother had been there to intervene and make us understand that professional ambitions are so much baloney when compared to things that really count for something, like being healthy and alive.

The story in the *Record* about what happened to Mandy was simple enough, but the aftereffects of the cupboard whiskey made it seem complicated and Shorty's coffee was perking inside me like something from a glass beaker in a cheapo sci-fi flick. The trouble with knowing better is that it never does me a bit of good. What made it worse was knowing that someone I used to love was dead and not being able to concentrate on what it meant. So I just kept staring at the blurred picture of Mandy O'Hare and the smudge where Shorty had put his thumb.

"I hadda laugh, a rich brat like her," Shorty was saying. "Imagine gettin' herself killed in a fleabag motel like that? And just when her old man is tryin' to get himself elected. Hey, I almost forgot, dint you know her or something, a long time back?"

A long time back. Hearing him put it that way made a little shiver go through me. I fished in my purse for a buck, put it on the counter, and left Shorty's place. Outside in the street the sunlight had broken through the gray overcast and shone like a white beacon over the city.

As I headed for the police station, I remember thinking that so much daylight all at once was cruel and unusual punishment.

Chapter Two

Truman Hawkins was at the station. He was sitting on a wooden bench in the front room, consulting a steno pad. He was chewing on a pencil and looking thoughtful. His bony forehead swelled out above his small triangular face and the slight protuberance of his eyes made them look large and froglike.

I sat down next to him and waited for the eyes to drift my way. Hawkins had interviewed me for an article in the *Record* shortly after I'd come home in disgrace. He'd played down the disgrace angle, for which I was thankful. Since then we'd crossed paths occasionally and once when drunk he'd propositioned me and been refused, a fact we'd both since chosen to ignore.

"What happened to Mandy, Truman?"

"Stabbed," he said. "Steak knife."

I was used to Hawkins's shorthand, which seemed to be verbalized directly from his steno pad. He actually took notes in Gregg, which impressed me. None of the sports reporters who'd interviewed me on the tour used the Gregg method. Many of them seemed to resist writing in English.

"Who killed her, Tru? Was it Bernardi?"

He squinted at me, worrying the stub of his pencil. "I'll trade you," he said. "I'll tell you the name of the accused if you'll tell me what you're doing here asking me."

"Oh God." I got up from the bench and looked around for someone who could answer a simple question.

"Do you have a client, Miss Kale?" Hawkins asked.

"What I've got," I told him, "is a headache."

The desk sergeant told me Detective Stein was probably down in Files. He was willing to go look, so long as I promised not to go in myself. Only police officers were allowed in the file room. Before he got back, a voice came up behind me.

"Hi, Connie."

I could tell by the way his eyes rolled that Detective Stein was glad to see me.

"What the Christ are you doing here?" he whispered. "Don't tell me you've already got a client on this?"

"Okay, I won't. As a matter of fact I don't. You know I haven't had a client in five months. You also know I don't care if another one doesn't come along for the next five years."

The part about not having a client was true. The rest was smoke.

"Okay, okay," he said, then added, grinning the grin he wore to bed. "So how exactly may I help you?"

Richard Stein was one of four detectives on the Rivermuth Police Department. He'd come to Maine by way of Teaneck, New Jersey, and a little of that was still left in his voice. He'd gotten married along the way. I'd had something going with him, against my better judgment, after he'd convinced me that the marriage was on the rocks. Lately his marriage seemed to be wedging itself off whatever rocks had originally imperiled it and I was beginning to think the only real rocks were the ones in my head.

5

"Can you tell me who did it?" I asked, trying to ignore the suggestive grin. "Was it Bo Bernardi?"

Stein relaxed his smile. He took my elbow and steered me into his office. He was careful to shut the door and I took the cup of coffee he offered.

"Funny you should think of Bo," he said. "That was my first reaction. But no, as I told Truman and everyone else, we are holding one Tony Steel, an exotic dancer who bills himself as The Man of Steel. Clever, eh? I'm reasonably sure that's not his real name, but that's all we have so far. He's clammed up."

"Steel?" There was something familiar about the name.

"Yeah. He's a male stripper booked from a sleazy outfit in Portland. From what we know he picked up Mandy at the Play Pen Club last night, where he and a couple of other guys were in this so-called All-Male Revue. Anyhow, our boy Tony took her to the Sea Breeze Motel. She was stabbed to death there and he was picked up at the scene at ten minutes to six this morning. One of the maids called us. That's really all I can give you now, Connie. You know how it is."

"Sure I do. God, I can hardly believe it. Mandy O'Hare?"

"I know. Pudge is out of town on some campaign thing, so the old man himself came down to identify the body."

The old man was Alfred O'Hare, Sr., usually referred to as The Governor on account of the one term he had served shortly after the Second World War. His son Pudge, AKA Alfred O'Hare, Jr., was Mandy's father and also a current candidate for a vacated seat in Congress. Lately I'd seen a lot of his slick campaign ads saturating the airways around the news slots. Now, I supposed, there would be a special edge to his run for Congress. Unless, of course, he decided to withdraw from the primary.

6

Richard looked skeptical when I mentioned that.

"You've got to be kidding," he said. "The Governor won't stand for it. He's been pushing Pudge into this for years. Continuing the proud family tradition and all that crap."

I wasn't sure it was crap, but didn't care to discuss it with Stein. There were parts of Richard that were solid cop, and politics was one of them. His idea of charisma was a check artist with nerve enough to use a fountain pen. My own feeling about the O'Hares was a little more complicated. There was a time when, at first because of my father's connection to the family, and later because of my friendship with Mandy, I had seen a lot of the clan, from the kind of intimate perspective reserved for children.

"Look, Connie," Richard was saying. "You know I'm always glad to see you. But I'm wondering exactly why you're here, you know?"

He was looking at me narrowly and something in his expression made me think I could read his thoughts, and he mine. I could feel the blood rising in my cheeks.

No one, not even Mandy, had ever believed me when I said I didn't hold it against her for taking my former husband to bed. She had engineered a seduction on New Year's Eve, in my own house, in full view of a company of friends. After that it was hard to explain that the marriage had already failed to take and that the game Mandy played was not even the last straw, it was merely a small sad exclamation point to a mistake that took two years correcting. No, I'd never held it against her. Mandy always did have a keen sense of timing.

Now Richard looked away from me until the flush passed. After a few moments of grace, he leaned back at his desk, hung that big grin on his face and said, "I'm assuming you'd tell me if you're working on this one."

I let that go for a moment. "Sure," I said. "You can

assume that. Besides, you've got the killer. There's no case, right?"

I was surprised when he ignored that. Instead he stood up and walked around to my side. "I don't care if you do nose around, Connie. You know how I feel about you. If it was up to me I'd open the files, let you at 'em."

"You're a charming liar, Richard."

He grinned an acknowledgment and took my empty cup.

"Well, at least I'm charming. Give me a couple of days on this, Con. When we have it nailed down, I'll fill you in on the gory details."

At that moment I wasn't interested in gory details and hoped I never would be. Richard stood behind me as I reached to open the door, his hands lightly touching my hips. I neither moved away nor encouraged him. Once we'd come close to having sex right there in his office, but today he wasn't about to risk it. It was all part of a continuing trend and I was reasonably certain his flirting now was more out of habit than desire.

"A favor, Dick?"

"Depends."

"I want to look at the guy."

His hands tightened on my hips, then melted away. "I guess there's no harm in that. Just a lookie, though—no talkie."

He took me to the elevator and down into the basement, where the detainee cells were located. The patrolman on duty knew better than to question Stein and he pretended to busy himself, studying a nightschool manual. But I was aware of him watching and listening as Stein guided me to the far end of the wall that enclosed the cell block.

The men on the force called the place the Dungeon with good reason. The foundation walls were set in uneven, rectangular chunks of granite. A section of the wall, in contrast to the old stonework, was cast in concrete, damp and cool to the touch. In the center of this, at eye level, was a sliding metal screen. Behind the screen was a slot about four inches high and a foot wide.

Stein lifted up the latch and slid back the metal screen. It was on a greased track, and noiseless.

"In case we need to keep an eye on a detainee," he explained. "You'd be surprised the guys try to hang themselves for getting popped in the drunk tank."

The panel of glass was thick. I assumed it was mirrored on the opposite side because it gave the small cell a bluish pall.

He was sitting on a cot, his arms hugging his knees. He was in profile to me and I could see that his skin was smooth and dark and his eyelids were heavy and well formed. A regular Sicilian dreamboat. His head pivoted toward the observation slot, and my impression, as our eyes locked, was that he looked exactly like a murderer.

Chapter Three

The bluff is a low, broad table of upthrust granite, topped with a few inches of pale soil. The Atlantic chips away at the base there and over the millennia has managed to drag enough sand from it to form beach dunes to the east and west. The bluff is now called Sankaty Head and has been for some three hundred years. Before that the Abenakis knew it as Mendosaquoi, which roughly translates to White Buttock. Some of the more droll locals still call the place White Fanny. This is not out of homage to the native Americans who named it, but out of envy of the four or five families who presently own the bluff and who maintain, at their own expense, the gated, blacktopped road that curves through the estates of Sankaty Head. There is a stone guard building at the east entrance, but the practice of keeping a guard on duty was dropped long ago. The little vine-covered building is empty now and the stained-glass windows I remember as a girl were removed, years before, to the chapel where Mandy O'Hare was about to receive last rites.

I left my car at the old guard building and walked. It

had been years since I traversed the Head on foot and I wanted to feel the place under me. The vast lawns of each estate are meticulously maintained, of course—acres of sodded turf that were brought in and unfurled like carpet. But on the road you can feel the bedrock, the bones of the place. You have the feeling that a time will come when the sea will again sweep over the bluff, carrying away the uprooted vegetation that has been so carefully nurtured by succeeding generations of gardeners and landscape architects.

My father is, or rather was, the greenskeeper at the Sankaty Head Golf Course, which in those days was wholly owned by the O'Hare Development Corporation. As a result of that and a kind of intimacy he had with Alfred O'Hare, Sr., he and my mother were given permission to be married in the chapel there. As a girl I adored looking at tinted photographs of the event, which depicted my parents and their friends as having once been absurdly young, dressed up almost like children at a costume party in suits and dresses a little oversized. I was absolutely certain that I, too, would be married in that chapel. I was right, but the marriage wasn't.

The funeral service was not largely attended. There were less than a dozen cars and only three limousines in the gravel lot behind the chapel, which is conveniently adjacent to the small, Catholic cemetery where several of the more recently deceased O'Hares are planted. They put Mandy next to her brother, the third of the Alfreds, called Alfie when I knew him. As a boy he had been small boned and delicate, his melon-shaped head too large for his frail body. In adolescence everything below his dimpled chin inflated and he became fat, padded with layers of beer and vodka. He never got to be an adult, having piled his Porsche into an overpass abutment at the Rivermuth traffic circle a few months before his twenty-first birthday. There was no question of suicide. He was just extremely drunk and lost his way.

Alfie and I were the same age and there was one summer when he was sweet on me. We were about eight, and I remember the china-blue eyes, round and protuberant in that large, tender head of his, woefully beseeching me not to make fun of his broken heart. Not that I broke it. No, I was perfectly willing to receive a small bunch of crushed geranium blossoms from the Governor's hothouse, although I was probably more interested in the Hershey kisses he carried in his small vest pocket. We were both wearing knee stockings, he in navy blue shorts and I in a linen dress, a dress worn specifically to summer Mass. I still have the sun bonnet that went with the dress. The dried flower blossoms my mother pinned to the rim have disintegrated, like a lot of other things.

Seeing the stone that marked Alfie's place, I couldn't help but remember what a timid boy he'd been and how Mandy, who was about to join him, had dominated him. The Governor had tried to overwhelm Alfie's wilting tendencies by exhorting him to athletic prowess. His father, Alfie was reminded by the Governor, had also been a sickly child. And it was a fact that Pudge, slightly lamed by polio, had built himself into a formidable athlete. Yes, from weakling to regional boxing champion! Defender of the O'Hare fortunes! Slayer of dragons! Poor Alfie responded by vigorously building himself up into the most prodigious and dutiful teenage alcoholic at the Head, and not without stiff competition from several cousins.

All of this had more to do with grandfather than father, if my childhood impressions are correct. In those days Pudge was like a gentle giant. When he wasn't busy managing the company, he might loom down now and again to bestow some beneficence on his children or on all the children who roamed the five estates in the summer months. He treated me, daughter of a mere greenskeeper, with none of the condescension I frequently encountered from the other parents and even from the servants, who were as keen on social distinctions as their employers.

Some of the old affection welled up again as I saw Pudge, older now and no longer the giant of my childhood, standing there by the chapel steps looking empty and confused. My first impression was that he was still an imposing and crudely handsome man. The Governor stood beside him, slightly taller and not so broad shouldered; his back was still ramrod straight and his thinning white hair scooped straight back on his sunbrowned bullet of a head.

I looked around for Bo Bernardi, whom Mandy had lately married for reasons obscure to her circle of acquaintances and perhaps even to Bernardi himself. I almost missed him because he had been excluded from the high ground where the O'Hare men stood, heads bowed. Bo was wearing a checked sports jacket, evidently borrowed from someone a size or two smaller than he because three or four inches of pale wrist showed below the cuffs.

I entered the gates hesitantly, not wanting to draw attention, since no one had bothered to invite me. I needn't have worried. As far as the clan was concerned, I was invisible. Or so I thought until a low voice mumbled, to the left and just behind me.

"Why, hello. Connie Kale, isn't it?"

I turned to find Dr. Sutcliffe hoveringin a shadow under an elm. He looked as wraithlike as ever. As a child I'd imagined he was made of soft rubber, without any bones at all. He gave me his hand, as cool and as moist as the earth under our feet.

"How is your father these days? I've been meaning to stop in."

"He's fine, considering. As mean as ever."

My father had, the previous year, suffered the stroke that put him in the wheelchair and deprived him of his voice. I knew he would prefer not to see Dr. Sutcliffe, whom he had always loathed, and I think Sutcliffe was aware of that.

"Terrible waste, isn't it," he said, making conversation. As the Governor's brother-in-law he was tolerated but not encouraged, especially in family situations like funerals or weddings, although I did recall him being summoned on more than one occasion to administer intravenous tranquilizers to Mandy's mother and later to Mandy herself. So he had his uses. "I hadn't seen the child in several months. Not since Bo happened. I'd thought she was getting on so well."

"Someone killed her," I reminded him. "Mandy didn't do herself in."

This was a distinction it was not always possible to make in reference to the departure of an O'Hare. Dr. Sutcliffe looked doubtful. "I suppose you're right," he said. "Still . . ." The word hung there, like the unfinished peal of a chapel bell.

I saw Dick Stein outside the gate to the cemetery and almost laughed. No doubt he thought he was fulfilling a professional requirement of some sort. Looking for suspicious types, lurking in trenchcoat and low brimmed hat, or whatever. He waved and I responded with what I hoped was a very cool smile.

I could see the Governor looking me over from the steps as he and Pudge waited for the pall bearers to position the casket. I'm quite sure he couldn't place me. I preferred it that way for the moment. Actually I didn't know exactly what I was doing there. It wasn't affection for Mandy because she couldn't know, nor would she have cared. Maybe it was nostalgia for those few summers at Sankaty Head, before things went bad.

Dr. Sutcliffe decided to attach himself to me. Probably it was a relief to talk to someone not of the family, indeed not even related to any of the five estates that were his sole practice. He was like a pale and distinguished, if somewhat funereal, limpet and I didn't have the heart or the energy to unfasten him.

"Pudge is taking it terribly hard, you know," he said, as if Pudge were a mutual friend of ours. "She was the light of his eye, that girl."

"Where's Kitty?" I asked, more out of politeness than curiosity. Kitty was now the sole survivor of the third generation. It was a morbid thought, and I wondered how long she would last, since she was at least as wild and flighty and given to instant gratification as Mandy had been.

"I had to give her a little something," said the good doctor, not without satisfaction. "She was hysterical, saying the most dreadful things to poor Pudge. As if it were his fault, you know."

I could still feel the iron gaze of the Governor smiting us both. Perhaps he suspected that Sutcliffe was babbling family secrets. Or maybe he could read lips. Or it might be that he just felt like exercising his glare. There was something about the way he stood there, as if rooted to the chapel steps, that made me want never to cross him. Unfortunately I have a bad habit of not following my own best instincts.

"I expect Bo feels rather awkward," said the doctor.

All I knew about Bo Bernardi was what I'd read in the papers, under "Police Report" and "Court Log." He owned a small garage that specialized in motorcycle repair, was something of a mascot to the local chapter of the Iron Horsemen, and had made a specialty of disturbing the peace. Usually he practiced this in a barroom or a restaurant and now and then charges were pressed—hence his fairly frequent appearances in court. His nose was unbroken and his features so delicate that I assumed his brawls were more noise than fist. The Rivermuth police, who knew him professionally, so to speak, considered Bo a harmless pain in the ass.

He didn't need an alibi because the case against Tony

Steel was very strong, but had he needed one his witness for the defense would be none other than Detective Stein himself. Stein had Bo under arrest for simple assault the night Mandy was murdered. Something to do with an altercation at the New Dolphin Lounge. Very convenient, in a morbid way.

As far as I knew, Bo Bernardi had been married to Mandy at the time of her death, legally, that is. They were no longer living together. I'm not sure they ever did. So he had reason to look awkward. Not the least of the reasons, as Sutcliffe promptly informed me, was that he was due to inherit a not inconsiderable sum from her estate. An oversight on Mandy's part, apparently. I know she had always hated lawyers and liked to string them along like puppies after sausage, never quite playing by the rules and never entirely violating them.

However much he was due to get, it wasn't enough to shield Bo from the palpable vibrations the Governor was exuding. Bo looked more than awkward. He looked frightened.

"He used to rough her up, you know," said Dr. Sutcliffe. "Black eyes, a sprained wrist. Oh, I treated her several times. Which is not to say I blame him entirely. She was a very spirited girl."

That was a nice way of putting it.

The priest, whom I did not recognize, was dragging his skirts through the grass, several paces behind the casket, which was being moved toward a gash in the earth. He was young, too young to be bidding goodbye to the dead, and on his unlined face I thought I detected an expression of nervous distaste. Not at saying a funeral Mass for a lost lamb like Mandy, but because he was not an intimate of the Sankaty Head Catholics, having been brought in, I supposed, from the Rivermuth diocese. I am not of the Church, although my mother was, and I guess you inherit some of it, because I involuntarily bowed my head as he prayed, first in Latin and then in English. Out of the corner of my eye, I noticed that Dr. Sutcliffe, who was most assuredly not a Catholic, felt free to watch the others as they prayed. He may or may not have been smiling.

Both of us had hung back from the entourage and when the small gathering began to disintegrate I found that he had vanished. I had the unkind thought that he might have returned to stick another needle in Kitty, into that delicious little rump of hers.

"That guy gives me the creeps," said Stein. He was waiting in the gravel parking lot, hip up on the fender of his unmarked cruiser. The O'Hare party had left through the graveyard, taking a slate-lined path that leads directly to their estate. "He reminds me of Uriah Heep, you know?"

I said I did. He offered me a ride back to my car. I told him I preferred to walk. It was nothing personal, I just wanted the exercise and the time to myself.

I slipped out of my heels and padded along in no hurry, the tarmac cool under bare feet. So far as I know, it is the only road in that part of southern Maine where elm trees still arch their voluminous boughs overhead, not one or two trees, but dozens of them. I'd heard my father scoff at the unheard-of sum that had been squandered to inoculate the trees against disease. Actually I think my father admired the White Fannies for spending the money; I know he loved elms and had refused to cut down the skeleton stump of one in our backyard. Finally the wind had done it for him, and taken out the summer porch in the process.

One of the limousines rolled by, moving only a little faster than I. The green canopy of elms was reversed in the deep black lacquer. The windows were blank and dark, but I felt someone watching from inside. The limo slowly accelerated, fat tires hissing, and passed around the curve out of view. Along the road was a neatly mortised stone wall, about shoulder height, and I could remember running along it once, pursued by another small child, or maybe chasing him. I was about to pass by a gate in the wall when I heard someone call my name. For a moment I thought it was Alfie, or rather something left of him that still roamed the gardens.

It was Dr. Sutcliffe, hurrying along the path. His left hand was up, clawing at the air in what I supposed was a sign of greeting or urgency, maybe both.

"Connie? Oh yes, it *is* you. How nice. I misplaced you somehow." Despite his hurrying he did not seem to be out of breath. "You see, the Governor would like to invite you back to the house."

Sutcliffe saw my puzzlement and smiled. His dentures were slightly askew and he straightened them un-selfconsciously with two forefingers before saying, "Come along, young lady. As you can see, I don't bite very well these days. You'll be quite safe with me."

Chapter Four

I wasn't so sure about there being no bite left in the old gentleman, although Sutcliffe was charming enough as he escorted me through the formal gardens, strewn with the last somber blossoms of autumn, and up toward the main house. Mostly he talked about my father and the good old days in and around the golf course and club house.

"He had quite a nimble sense of humor, Johnny Kale did."

"He still does," I reminded him, uneasy to have my father so easily relegated to the past tense. The doctor gave me one of his significant looks.

Although it had been some fifteen years since I last entered the O'Hare mansion, I remembered the layout clearly enough to know that Dr. Sutcliffe was not taking me in by the usual access, that is, through the kitchens or in from the stables. When I veered that way he tugged at my purse strap, muttered something, and guided us around the great porches that faced the sea. I noticed that the drapes had been drawn across all the windows on the lower floor.

"The library, you know," said the doctor, fluting through his nose, "More convenient and so on."

The entrance to the library was secluded, a mere gap between evergreen hedges. Once inside, Dr. Sutcliffe immediately melted through an inner door, leaving me alone. It was a room I had never been in before; no doubt it was forbidden to children and casual guests.

The ceiling was a good twelve feet high, higher than in the rooms I remembered in the rest of the house. The paneled wall facing the sea was slightly oval. Later I was told that the library, one of several additions to the main house, had been designed by the late Byron O'Hare, the Governor's brother, and built under his supervision by a crew of cabinet makers from one of the old woodworking shops in Camden. That explained the gentle curve of the multipaned windows and the dark teak shelves that hold one of the largest private collections on landscape architecture. In addition to bound vellum tomes issued by Frederick Law Olmsted, Pierre Charles L'Enfant, and others whose names I did not recognize, there were several chamois-bound volumes on modern land use by Byron O'Hare himself. I was just cynical enough to wonder if he hadn't designed the entire library around their display.

Not that the library housed only books. It was a much more tactile place than that; I couldn't resist tracing my fingers over the meticulous scale models of housing developments, which were so realistically constructed they made me feel as if I were looking down from a great height. One of the walls was composed of framed photographs, illuminated by cove lights. Several of the pictures were of "Balicourt," the first of Byron's big developments, completed before he and his brother decided to move the family seat to Sankaty Head from Long Island, where their immigrant father had made the business of growing small potatoes a relatively large and prosperous enterprise.

At present there seems nothing particularly remarkable about the idea of linking modular home construction to golf courses, tennis courts, and recreational zones, but in 1948 the O'Hare Development Corporation was one of the first to promote the concept. In retrospect, all you have to do is option a few square miles of pasture within forty miles of an urban center, carve out a golf course, season with an artificial lake or two, garnish with twelve hundred units of housing, and let your investment bake for about ten years. When you pull that little suburban cupcake out of the oven you will have enlarged the family fortune four- or five-hundredfold, and your father's potato fields will be forever buried under patchworks of green lawn and blacktop. You almost expected to see giant green dollar signs worked into the landscape of the "Balicourt" photograph.

When the O'Hares established themselves at Sankaty Head, the two brothers had optioned land directly adjacent to it. This was now the golf course where my father had worked, and in one of the aerial photographs I spotted the house where I had grown up. By squinting I imagined I could make out my old swingset, long since rusted into the ground. Alongside this was an enlarged snapshot of Byron and Alfred with Winthrop "Windy" Browning, the club pro. According to the caption the threesome had won a local match; they looked terribly young and unreasonably happy.

The pictures of Byron ceased abruptly in 1952 and when they resumed again Byron had been replaced by his brother's son. Now it was Pudge, younger and darker and always grinning that lopsided O'Hare grin as he was caught in the act of cutting ribbons, shoveling spades of earth, placing cornerstones, or posing at the first tee of a new development, ready to open the course and unleash the sales campaign all in one swing.

And it was Pudge who was the subject of one of the oils that was the original for the September 1960, cover of *Time* magazine, with its special section of suburban development and that bold new idea, condominiums. A little arithmetic told me that Pudge's sister Louise was still alive when the magazine hit the stands and his wife Elisha had not yet begun her series of trips to the bin where she was now in permanent residence. Rosier times, on the whole. I wondered if it was fortitude he'd inherited from the Governor (who was strangely absent from the photographs) or just good skin.

"Miss Kale?"

I had just a glimpse of Dr. Sutcliffe hovering behind Alfred O'Hare, Sr. When the doors slid closed on oiled tracks Sutcliffe was gone and I was alone with the Governor.

"Will you join me, Miss Kale?"

He went to a cabinet that was built under the architect's scale model of "Serenity," the mountain retreat Byron had not lived long enough to finish. He showed me a dark green bottle. I told him it was a little early for me.

"Nonsense, my dear girl. Our little Mandy was herself a cognac drinker. Among other things." He poured two small portions into rocks glasses. I was grateful not to be handed one of those foolish crystal balloons. "To Mandy?" he said.

I was about to be charmed. There was a brightness about the eyes, which were directed into my own, a kind of intimate posture of the prodigious O'Hare jaw. There was a definite sense of familiarity being established, as if it were important that I know I was being charmed and would willingly accede to it.

"Now then. Our little Kitty tells me you're in the detective business. Is that correct?"

I shrugged. "Sherlock Holmes was a detective. I've tried, but I can't smoke a calabash pipe. So what I do is sometimes I assist in an investigation."

"You assist in an investigation. Sometimes."

I had a feeling he was feeding the words back to me to

22

see how I liked them. I wasn't sure I did, or how I felt about being pegged by sister Kitty.

"So what happened to the promising career in golf?" he asked. I detected no hint of sarcasm, and possibly a genuine ignorance of the details of my abortive career. "Last thing I remember your Dad was announcing that his little Constance had qualified for the tour. I'm a little vague about what happened after that."

I was a little vague about it myself, but I took a hot sip of the cool-to-the-touch cognac and cranked up for the standard version. How, after winning a number of amateur tournaments in New England I'd been offered an athletic scholarship to Rollins College in sunny Florida. How I'd captained the golf team there and on the strength of that been admitted into the Women's Professional Golf Tour instructional school. How I'd gotten my card and slugged my way through one very depressing year, continually discovering that I didn't have the right stuff. How I'd just happened to be there in Atlanta when Jo Ann Ritzer, the season's high money winner, had been kidnapped and how, mostly through dumb luck, I'd helped secure her release and thereby earned enough reward money to more than make up for what I'd lost in that dismal season on tour. How, now and again, I tendered quiet assistance in similar investigations, usually but not always connected to the world of professional sports, and frequently managed, as part of the agreement, to keep it out of the papers.

As I droned on, boring myself, I got the impression the Governor was familiar with most of it after all, because he was nodding in all the right places and was obviously waiting for me to finish. The only time his eyes lit up was when I mentioned keeping things out of the papers.

"Very interesting," he said, cutting me short before I'd quite wrapped up the standard version. "I didn't ask you in here as an investigator, Connie," he continued, "but as a friend of the family."

This was so ludicrous I almost burst out laughing. I was pretty sure he had not remembered my name until Dr. Sutcliffe supplied him with it. It was also possible that he had forgotten the slight intimacy he had once had with my father. But I am not immune to the considerable attractions of power and wealth as specifically embodied in a once famous and still virile man of seventy-five, or of any particular age for that matter. So I knocked back the sweet liquor and waited, my curiosity aroused.

"I'll be blunt, Connie. The sad truth is I gave up on Mandy a number of years ago. You may think me a heartless old man, but right now—today—my chief concern is how all this may affect Pudge. His chance."

His dismissal of Mandy was hardly a surprise. Most everyone who had ever known her, blood kin or not, had given up on her at one time or another. Now that she was dead the cut was final. There would be no petitions from that peaceful little grave under the elms.

"I'm referring to the campaign, of course. I needn't remind you that it has been a long time coming. Pudge turns fifty-two this year and up until now he has always resisted involving himself in politics. My own failed example has 'turned him off' as you young people say." He looked down into the glass, possibly to examine his own reflection. "The fact is that if Mandy had to die it would have been better for all concerned if she'd found a more conventional way of doing so."

For the second time that day I found myself reminding a member of the family that Mandy had not done herself in.

"I suppose not," agreed the Governor. "But it amounts to the same thing. She was risking her life, mucking about in dives like that, with men like him. Remember that our little Mandy actually went and married that grease monkey Bernardi." His voice rose in indignation. "What kind of name is that for a white man? Do you know he has tattoos on his arms? And God knows where else. And then the little brat goes off to some wretched motel with a male prostitute! Something awful was bound to come of it."

Somehow or other he'd maneuvered us into opposite chairs, to one side of an enormous and empty mahogany desk. The Governor was lighting my cigarette. He didn't smoke, but like all politicians, no matter for how long out of office, he carried a lighter.

"So you see I must be practical. Pudge is, frankly, in shock. Mandy was very special to him. I don't believe he ever fully understood what she has been up to all these years. What father could? She went off the track when she was about fourteen, you know."

I knew, but didn't say so. I wondered if the Governor knew what had happened between Mandy and my former husband and concluded that he probably did. Not that he was likely to mention it; if he used the knowledge at all it would be as an invisible lever. I admit that at the time, sitting there in that grand library, I found the process of being manipulated by the likes of Alfred O'Hare pretty fascinating.

"But let's not speak ill of the dead. She *was* my granddaughter, although I don't believe she had much of my blood. Or Pudge's. Her mother, you know."

I understood how important blood and lineage could be to a man whose grandfather had scrambled for blighted potatoes before escaping the famine by emigration.

"How closely have you been following the campaign?" he asked. He stood up and walked toward the curved windows, leaving me in the chair. When he turned back I could no longer see his face.

"Just what I read in the papers. It's not going too well, according to the polls."

The former governor dismissed polls with a judo chop

of his hand. "Smoke," he insisted. "Democratic smoke. But I'll let you in on a little secret, Connie. Pudge and I never expected to win this one. There is a chance Pudge may take the primary, but the seat itself is untouchable this year. I repeat, *this* year. However, two years from now Pudge can run again and it will be along with the President. An enormous difference in a presidential election year, do you follow me? National prestige on the line. The Party will get behind us. They need someone of caliber and class representing this state. Someone who knows how to carry himself . . ."

And so on. It was a speech, not a conversation. Even after almost thirty years Alfred O'Hare was still burning for office, this time through the vehicle of his son's career. In the early fifties Alfred O'Hare had come from behind in a three-way race to win the highest office in the state of Maine. After one controversial term he had failed to regain his party's nomination, had then waged furious battle as an independent candidate, and had lost handily. The bid as an independent had ruined him forever with his party. That had not prevented his running for nomination every two years, always a voluble loser, always good copy (so the old boys at the *Record* told me) for two decades. That he never became a joke was due entirely to his furious charm and to the fact that in election after election no one was absolutely sure he would not win.

As he stood there, silhouetted against the windows, I knew he was talking more to himself than to me. A pep talk in the face of the latest tragedy. That was his way, his tradition, and I almost admired him for it.

"I'm sure you see the implications here, Connie. There will be publicity, very ugly publicity. There are those who will try to smear him with what happened to Mandy, that he was a poor father, a bad example. Reputation is so easily lost . . ."

Despite having a pretty good idea where all this was

leading, I was taken aback by the naked way he put the proposition.

"What we need, what we absolutely require if we're going to manage this campaign with any kind of style, is an informant. Someone who can clue us into whatever ugly little things the police may uncover and let us know about it before the media—not to mention Pudge's opponents—can formulate an effective attack."

I must have blanched because he quickly cleared his throat and altered the slightly venomous timber of his voice.

"Nothing illegal, mind you. Just an extra edge. Just information a little before anyone else gets it. I mean that all *does* come under the heading of investigation, does it not?"

I managed to nod. "I wouldn't have put it exactly that way, sir. But I'm forced to admit it's all part of the process."

The Governor had come back out of the light toward the mahogany desk. He braced himself against it with the physical ease of a much younger man.

"I wouldn't dream of interfering in whatever it is you do, Constance. Naturally we would pay the going rate—if you have no objections I may list you under campaign expenses as a media consultant—and there would be only one restriction."

I lifted my eyebrows by way of inquiry, my mouth too dry for speech.

"That is," he said gently, "that you report directly to me."

Chapter Five

The main street in Rivermuth, Maine, is called Maine Street. I've always assumed the founding fathers were poor spellers rather than weak punsters, but maybe I'm selling them short.

Some years ago the elms that marked the boundaries of the street died and it was widened and "improved," in much the same spirit that the neighborhoods were improved in the fifties, by urban removal. But Maine still winds slowly through the heart of the city, passing the new government complex and the old bus depot, then gradually sloping downward toward the eastern waterfront, into that part of town where blank neon tubes are bent over dull brick facades. There the porn shops and the peep shows and the massage parlors come and go at the whim of whoever happens to own the city council.

The Play Pen Club is a one-story, cinderblock building situated in a parking lot next to the wharves. The plate-glass storefront has been painted black ever since I can remember, and on the mottled surface are the remains of boldly drawn cartoon figures of impossibly busty women attired in bunny costumes from another era. It was a trend that has long since been erased by a succession of strippers, belly dancers, go-go girls, wet tee-shirt girls, and mud-wrestling girls. And lately, naked boys who dance, to put as polite a label on it as possible.

Near the entrance a few square feet of the black paint had been scraped away and it was there I saw the poster, taped to the glass from the inside.

ALL-MALE REVUE
Triple Threat Star Attractions
presenting
RANDY THE ROGUE! TONY STEEL!
MAXIMUM JON!
$3 Cover   Ladies Only

There is no lack of dark corners in the Play Pen and I took a table in one of them. Waiting for a drink I experienced a kind of skewed nostalgia. The Pen had been one of the forbidden denizens of my adolescence, when it had been a thrill to join a group of hell-raising, underage girls who thought it a distinct pleasure to drink diluted booze there and have their hearing blunted by the local imitators of the Beatles and the Rolling Stones. Part of the thrill was the chance to flirt with the rather seedy waterfront flotsam, none of whom ever looked remotely like Marlon Brando, no matter how blinded one was by the smoke.

That was years ago and I noticed that the old flakeboard ceiling had been pulled down, exposing black iron joists. I left my drink untouched on the table and decided the new ceiling was a distinct improvement, giving the dirty old Pen the trendy look of a renovated warehouse, so long as you ignored the peeling linoleum floor and the fake birch paneling that was beginning to buckle away from the cinderblock walls.

Many of the women who were pouring through the

doors, waving tickets and giggling amiably, had come directly from an office party at Liberty Fund, the big insurance headquarters out on the highway. They were pretty well primed. All in all the crowd temperament wasn't much different from what you might expect of an all-male audience at a county fair strip show.

It was different for me because I was working. Or so I kidded myself. Actually I was indulging curiosity. I have no objection to watching a man take his clothes off and had never had the chance to observe it under precisely these circumstances.

My attention was drawn to the stage where a slender young man with deep-set eyes appeared, holding a microphone.

"Just a quick word with you, ladies. As you may know, there is supposed to be three dancers appearing for your pleasure tonight. Due to circumstances beyond our control, two of these gentleman are not here . . ."

He was interrupted by a round of good-natured booing and some loud whistles.

". . . but that is gonna be okay, we still got one handy, dandy, randy dancer, and he's gonna do three shows for you girls and listen, you are gonna *love* it."

Comments I overheard from the Liberty Fund set tipped me to the fact that the radio ads pumping the revue, which had a run of ten days, had been careful not to mention the new solo aspect of the show. The sound system cut back in, louder than before, and after a minute or so the house lights went down.

A single blue spot wobbled on the small, slightly elevated stage. After a few thumping bars of the Stones' "Missed You," the same voice that had made apologies announced, in stagey breathlessness, "For your continuous pleasure, please welcome *Randy!*"

The same youth then appeared on stage, covering his deep-set eyes with mirrored sunglasses. He had changed to

30

a pair of loose cotton drawstring pants and was bare-chested. Around his neck was a red satin scarf. He began to dance energetically to the Stones, complete with enthusiastic hip action. I assumed he thought the smirk on his face was reminiscent of Mick Jagger. To give him credit he looked pale and wan enough to be Jagger, but spoiled it by being better looking.

As the Stones segued to a Lou Reed medley, he slipped out of the cotton trousers and pranced down off the stage, right up to the ropes that separated the narrow performance area from the arms and hands that waved inches from him. Now he was mugging Lou Reed and doing a pretty fair job of it, too. Shaping his tinted lips and rolling his eyes. Possibly gay, I thought, but with all the right equipment, which was barely contained by a bulging, sequined G-string. As he strutted by, shaking his ass, I thought he was just a little too pale and androgynous to interest me. Still, the rowdy contingent of paper pushers from Liberty Fund started hobbling their chairs and tables closer to the ropes, obviously interested in getting a closer look at what lay beneath the tick-tocking G-string. A woman in her mid forties, who looked like a typing pool super and probably a mother of four, shouted, "Baby, shake that meat!" amid hoots and cheers.

The dancer played into the sense of naughtiness. He rubbed himself up against the backs of chairs, almost but not quite touching the typists and key punchers who squealed there gleefully. I suspect the same women would have responded to a covert grope on a crowded bus by unleashing their hatpins and purses, but the blue spotlight following the lithe dancer seemed to have neutralized resistance, making anything permissible.

Randy was a professional of sorts, if not much of a dancer. He knew how to please a crowd, as he demonstrated by doing things with the red scarf that Gypsy Rose Lee never thought of. This seemed to be a generally understood signal because all over the room purses were opened and dollar bills began to appear in eager hands. Drinks were upset and tables jostled as the crowd clotted into the aisle, pressing against the ropes as the dancer hip-strutted by, snapping the elastic strap of his G-string to the beat of recorded music. His thighs were rigid, shining with oil and a sheen of sweat. Enameled fingernails, trimmed short for the rapid typing of insurance forms, stuffed crumpled bills into his G-string basket. The dancer tufted the ends of the bills out over his cup and I saw a few of the more daring hands actually reach inside the G-string to make their deposits, pausing just long enough to stroke the goodies before the dancer bobbed away, impish and apparently flaccid.

He timed his withdrawal to coincide with the end of one of the David Bowie tunes that was rattling the speakers, as well as the inside of my head. The lights came up immediately and in the brief intermission there was a rush for the bar and lines formed for the single stall of the women's room.

The prospect of sitting through two more shows was numbing. I decided to make my move. The dressing-room door was marked STORAGE, but I had seen the dancer duck inside and was reasonably sure there were no adjoining exits. I knocked firmly, trying to make my rat-a-tat sound friendly.

"Is that you, Bill?"

That was reason enough to open the door and lean in. Randy was wearing a robe and sitting on a stack of beer cases. He hastily concealed a joint when he saw me.

"Relax. I just wanted to pop in and say how much I loved the show."

Randy looked doubtful. His mascara was starting to smear and he looked like he needed sleep, if not a square meal. "Do I know you from somewhere? The beach?"

I closed the door behind me and leaned against it,

pasting on a smile I hoped was disarming. "No, you're just now making my acquaintance."

He shrugged and brought the joint out again. The theatricality of the gesture and his subsequent pose made me think that in another line of work Randy the Rogue might make a pretty fair journeyman actor, the type who plays effete villains or homicidal sadists. Not that he struck me as sadistic, exactly. It was the half-twisted smile that did it and eyes that were millimeters too close to the blade of his nose.

"You'd better state your business, dear," he said coolly, but not unpleasantly. "This is my rest time. I've got to go out again in thirty minutes. It may not look like work, but believe me, honey, it is."

"Must be pretty tough without Tony Steel, huh?"

The eyes hooded and he exhaled sharply. The smell of burning weed began to stifle me.

"What do you mean by that," he hesitated, "exactly?"

"I mean you have to carry the whole show on your own. Pretty tough. So what happened to the other guy, uh, 'Maximum Jon'?"

Randy made his lips smile. "You're being nosy, near. You don't by any chance actually *know* Maxy, do you? Or Tony?"

I thought of the Sicilian dreamboat behind blue glass. "I've seen Tony around," I said. "You know."

"Yeah, I know. Look, I'm really very tired. I'd like to be alone." He staged a yawn and curled the smile higher, showing me his canine teeth. I thought about a certain Doberman who had once tried to remove my ankle. It made me wonder if Randy was partial to baying at the moon.

Something pushed me violently forward, almost into Randy's naked lap. He was as surprised as I was and looked, for the briefest of moments, like a maiden whose honor had just been assaulted.

33

"Sorry, lady," said the big-gutted man who managed the club. "Hey, bubba," he said to Randy with more than a hint of menace in his flat, coastal drawl. "We gotta talk some. You agree we oughter talk?"

Randy made a noncommittal gesture. "Sure. Anything you say."

"Hey, you're what's-her-name; am I right? The girl detective or whatever?"

That hoisted my skirts, so to speak, and from the expression on Randy's powdered face he had no interest in what he saw there.

"That's not fair," he said, appealing to the manager who was backing from the room. "I spend hours and hours being grilled by those perfectly beastly cops and now this little bitch is trying to trick me."

"Nice trick," said the manager, leering. "Mighty fine." Randy kicked at the door after it shut.

"It's not as if *I* did anything," he said reproachfully, to no one in particular. He turned to me. "And you go straight to hell."

But there was not much conviction in the way he said "hell." It sounded like a club he had once worked and was now recommending.

"No tricks, Randy. See? Nothing up my sleeves. Just a few questions."

He slumped down on the stack of beer cases, looking morose and exhausted.

"It's always just a few questions," he sighed. "Thank *gawd* this is the last night in this toilet."

When Alfred O'Hare retained me he'd agreed to allow a wide latitude for investigation. The implication was that he wanted to know the ugly details before they could be used, in whatever twisted way, to smear Pudge's campaign. I had been treating Randy as an ugly detail. Now, for all his affectations, I was beginning to think he lacked the necessary ingredients for scandal. Nevertheless I had to go through the motions.

"Did you know Mandy O'Hare?"

He shook his head automatically. "No. I didn't know Mandy O'Hare. And to answer your next question, as far as I know Tony never knew the little slut until the night she picked him up. That's what I told the cops, over and over again, and that's what I'm telling you."

"What if I told you I was working for Tony Steel?" I said, making it up as I went along. Maybe I could appeal to a sense of camaraderie. Siblings of the G-string and so on.

But Randy looked amused. "Whatta you think, he's a friend of mine?" The upper lip curled again, and the eye teeth glistened. "No, you can't be working for Tony Steel or you'd know better."

He glanced at his bare wrist, as if expecting to find a watch there. "Look, baby doll, this isn't working for either of us. The cops had more questions, and better ones. Come to think of it they seemed like a horny bunch of bastards. Why don't you take your long legs down there and investigate with them? Maybe you could work out a trade or something."

Actually, it wasn't a bad idea.

Chapter Six

Jesus Christ was looking neglected. Her long arms drooped over the wooden stake where I had pinned her, and her green-leaved head was brittle and dull. I watered her roots and sprinkled a token of Miracle-Gro in her clay pot to appease my guilt. I could see the headlines, composed by Truman Hawkins: LOCAL INVESTIGATOR ARRESTED FOR ABUSE OF IRREVERENTLY NAMED AVOCADO PLANT. And in smaller type: MISS KALE OF WYBIRD STREET ACCUSED OF DELIBERATE HERBICIDE.

My lack of success with houseplants is probably a direct reaction to my father's professional reverence for anything green, whether golfed upon, clipped, or consumed with oil and vinegar. Jesus was the last survivor of the plants he'd given me when I'd settled into my Wybird Street digs. Her pitiful form was guilt inducing and I'd finally moved her out to the sunporch, hoping that the increase in radiation would either bring her back or finish her off. I put my second cup of coffee on the rickety porch table, arranging the files and notes on the O'Hare case in arbitrary piles.

It was Sunday and the "Mostly Mozart" program was on the Maine Public Broadcasting FM station. A light drizzle spattered against the windows of my little sunporch. I was content to be inside, alone, and working. The files that would occupy me for the morning had been supplied by Detective Richard Stein. Well, not exactly supplied. After much wheedling and the obligatory flirting that we both knew was contrived, he had agreed to leave me unattended in his office, where I used the small Savin copy machine to dupe the files he had accumulated on Mr. Tony Steel, AKA Anthony Alamia.

I'm a sap for dialogue. So it was natural that, sifting through the files and folders, I gravitated first to portions of the transcript containing Richard's interrogation of Tony Steel.

STEIN: Okay, Tony. Let's go over it again. If you really mean to cooperate we need details.

STEEL: Fine. You got 'em.

STEIN: So you're telling me that Mandy approached you in the Play Pen Club?

STEEL: The Pig Pen, that's what I'd call it. But yeah, she come up to the bar and asked me did I want a drink. This was after, so I was changed and cleaned up and just sort of relaxing, you know?

STEIN: You were observed by the bartender? When Mandy approached you?

STEEL: I guess so, sure. She was pretty easy on the eyes. I think the guy leaned in for a better look when he poured her drink. Why not?

STEIN: And you say she propositioned you?

STEEL: More or less.

STEIN: What do you mean more or less?

STEEL: I mean she kind of slipped her hand into my pants and gave me a honk, you know?

I sputtered the coffee and couldn't help but laugh. That sounded exactly like something Mandy would do. The transcript was more than a hundred double-spaced pages and pretty tedious, taken as a whole. I started skipping for parts that caught my eye.

> STEEL: I mean I hardly knew the girl, how could I? But, to be honest, the kid was kind of a screwball. I didn't see her that way immediate. It was later on I knew she was a flake. She had, you know, problems.

He wasn't what I would call well spoken, but a host of psychiatrists and counselors had, after vast expenditures of time and money, arrived at the same conclusion.

> STEIN: Okay, we'll follow up on that. Right now maybe you could fill in the background for me. You're employed as what, a dancer? Why don't you tell me a little about that.
> STEEL: Sure. Not much to tell. Like I said I met this guy Jon Maxfield while I was in—
> STEIN: This was in Thomaston? On the check forgery charge?
> STEEL: Yeah, they really shafted me on that. Anyhow this guy Maxie kind of took me under his wing. The guy knew the ropes and I didn't. Hey, I'll admit it, I was scared shit in there. Writing some bad paper is nothing, there was guys in there raped and killed their own mammas.
> STEIN: Yes, I'm sure there was. Let's stick to the present for now, Tony. How did you happen to get in this, ah, "business" you're in?
> STEEL: Like I say, that was Jonny Max. He knew this guy Arnold Maury out of Portland. Guy used to book big-time wrestlers. You ever heard of Doctor Nervo?

STEIN: I can't say I have.

STEEL: Well anyway he was a big-shot wrestler, on teevee, the whole bit. But that stuff kind of went down the tubes and this guy Maury started booking girlie acts. You know, wet tee-shirt contests and mud wrestling, in clubs all over New England. So Maxie set it up with him and then he asked me would I do it and I thought it over and said why not? The money is pretty good. Of course I cleared it with my parole officer first.

STEIN: What exactly is it you do?

STEEL: You probably think it's pretty weird, but what we do is take off our clothes and dance around and shake the old equipment in front of all these women. It's a fad thing right now, like mud wrestling used to be. I went into it with my eyes open. I mean I know it ain't going to last forever.

I thought about Randy in his threadbare robe, sweaty and exhausted. He didn't look like he was going to last forever, either. Mr. Alamia was a very chatty individual, whose use of the vernacular was probably much flatter in the transcripts than in person, from what Richard had told me about him. He went on about his booking agent, a small-time hoodlum named Arnold Maury, for about ten pages before Richard got him back to what happened to Mandy O'Hare.

STEEL: It was like, I don't know. Like suddenly she thought she was on this date with me. I mean once we got out of the bar she wants to hold hands. She's humming this little tune and looking up at the stars and giving me these shy little smiles. That's when I started thinking this broad has a screw loose. I mean she had been groping

39

me there in the Pen and now it's a honeymoon romance. But hey, I didn't mind. It was kind of nice, I guess, if you're into that sort of stuff.

The crude dialogue started to come alive for me as Tony told Richard Stein how Mandy had clung to his hand as they walked through the cool evening. A ground fog was laden with the scent of salt water; the tide was changing. Mandy had a small silver flask of cognac in her purse and she sipped from it as they walked, leaning her head against his broad shoulders. At her suggestion he carried her over the threshold and into the darkened motel room. She was, he told Stein, a light package.

Mandy poured the last of the cognac into two paper cups and then asked Tony to dance. Stein quickly ascertained that what she wanted from Tony was not a private strip show. What she wanted to do was waltz inside his arms. It was a crazy thing, he insisted, because Mandy had turned on one of those tiny Japanese tape decks, the kind no larger than a pack of cigarettes, and she had only one pair of headphones.

That was when I started to believe at least part of Tony Steel's story. I could well imagine Mandy O'Hare slow dancing to a song only she could hear.

After repeated prompting from Stein, Tony admitted to sharing a few lines of cocaine with Mandy. He insisted that the vial of powder had been Mandy's all along and that he had not sold it to her, that he had never dealt in cocaine or in any other drug. The traces of powder Stein's men found on the mirror left on the bureau had been hers, and Tony said she took most of the lines for herself.

Cognac and cocaine, and then an interlude of sex described by the stripper as "the regular sort of thing, nothing kinky." After which he'd fallen asleep. When he woke up Mandy was dead beside him and the knife that had pierced her heart was lying on the floor by the unlocked door, wiped clean of prints.

> STEIN: Come on, Tony. Can't you come up with something better than that? Who are you covering for?
>
> STEEL: Believe me I know how dumb that sounds. You think I wouldn't like to have a better story? But that's the truth, dumb as it is. I fell asleep or passed out and when I come to I had this blood all over my back where it had soaked into the mattress. Like I told you before, I freaked out. I mean, wouldn't you? I run into the bathroom and turned on the shower and washed it off. Right away I knew I was doing the wrong thing but I couldn't help it. So I put this towel around me and I ran out the door. There was this cleaning woman a couple of rooms over, with one of those cart things they pull around with mops and brooms and stuff. So she gets freaked—I scared her, I guess—and she starts hitting me with this broom and I'm yelling for her to call the cops. Finally that's what she did.

It was pretty sad, really. Even while being murdered Mandy had made a botch of things; what should have been a straight tragedy was starting to have elements of comedy. Quirky, futile comedy, the sort of thing opposing election campaigns can safely leak to the media. Alfred O'Hare was one of the least ridiculous of men and he wasn't going to like this one bit. He had hired a top-flight public relations outfit, and I assumed they would have their hands full tuning up Pudge's image as a doting father, recently bereaved over his strong-willed, totally independent daughter, with the emphasis on independent.

The thing of it was, it was probably true. I sifted through reams of the transcript, put aside an autopsy report, complete with diagrams, unopened. Richard had accumulated a wealth of material on Anthony Alamia, much of it related to his recent conviction for check forgery. I was a little surprised to see that it was his first felony conviction—or any conviction, for that matter. Doubtless that had a strong bearing on his being released after only six months, and on the unusually liberal terms of his parole.

Detective Stein had attached a paper clip to one page of transcript. It was his way of marking something worth further perusal and a little ghost of bent wire still adorned my photocopy.

> STEIN: And your friend Maxfield never showed up?
> STEEL: Right. He called Randy from the bus station in Portland and said he'd meet us down here. But like I say, he never showed.
> STEIN: Was Mr. Maxfield in the habit of missing these, ah, engagements of yours?
> STEEL: Well . . . Maxie wasn't what you'd call dependable, you know?

It was curious that Richard Stein had seen fit to flag the reference to "Maximum Jon" Maxfield. I tried reading between the imperfectly typed lines and found them as gray and blank as my own state of mind. So I tucked the Tony Steel file away and decided that the tough-guy dialogue had jagged my nerves in a way that Mozart couldn't fix.

There are certain instincts and habits that refuse to stay buried, no matter how hard you try. When my nerves are frayed I want to have a club in my hands; an odd perversity since it was the game that originally frayed my nerves. There was no use fighting it, so I went to the porch closet, pried open the door, and snaked out a putter. It was the same club that had betrayed me in Atlanta, and the bronze head reminded me of the copperhead snake my high school biology teacher kept in a jar of formaldehyde.

Without really meaning to I had settled into a stance on the threadbare carpet. Looming down over the little white ball, I closed my eyes and let go, sliding into a familiar trance of concentration and memory. I was back on the fourteenth green at Atlanta, one stroke away from making the cut. Most of the gallery had decamped to follow Jo Ann Ritzer to the next tee. Doubtless none of the stragglers who remained knew how important the putt was to the sagging career of Connie D. Kale. So there was no one to worry about. Nobody to blame but myself. Don't stab the ball, I thought, but the urgency was there and the rhythm had vanished and my wrists broke, pushing the ball instead of stroking it.

When I looked up with open eyes it had not only missed the hole I'd seen in my mind, it had carommed off a table leg and put a new crack in Jesus Christ's clay pot.

Unfortunately I don't believe in portents. If I had I would have gone directly to the phone and called the Governor to tell him I was off the case. All in all it might have been better that way.

Chapter Seven

The Birmingham must not have figured large in the various schemes of the O'Hare Development Corporation. The grounds, while lavishly maintained, are less than two acres. Its tenants have no adjacent golf course, or tennis courts, and have to make do with one Olympic-sized swimming pool.

Possibly the corporation had undertaken the project with an eye for favorable local publicity, since the Birmingham, a majestic old landmark from the Victorian era, was due to be flattened to make way for a three-tier parking lot. Not that the conversion of the grand old hotel into condos was in any sense a nonprofit operation. On the contrary, the great mass of brick and sandstone and leering gargoyles had been subdivided and refurbished at extravagant cost exceeded only by the margin of profit per unit.

Mandy had taken the penthouse. Whether she had paid the going rate was an interesting question. Knowing Mandy it was quite possible she had bullied her father into turning the keys over gratis; like many another poor little rich girl she was lavish with whatever she had in her pockets and tight as a drum otherwise. Still, the internecine squabbles that had erupted over her seizure of the best unit in the Birmingham were not within the parameters of the investigation. What I wanted was a last look inside Mandy's head and the only thing left of her was the place she'd lived in.

Alfred, as the Governor had asked me to call him, had given me the key and cautioned me to be discreet. I had an idea that hereafter our conversations would revolve around his rather fanatical idea of what discretion implied.

The condo parking spaces were patrolled by a security guard who looked like an unleashed, two-legged Doberman, so I squeezed my Duster into a slot a couple of blocks away, and walked. Shortly after the renovation was completed, I'd made the mistake of wandering into the en-marbled lobby for a look-see. In the back of my mind I had wanted to "bump into" Mandy again, if not to reinvoke our friendship then to pick up a quick charge of her energy. The only acquaintance I made that day was a condo sales-person, who spread himself over me like an oil slick. His spiel was full of phrases like "harmonically historical inte-riors" and "mood barometer" and "investment interface," and it had taken me a good twenty minutes of repeating the word "no" at regular intervals to scrape the slime off my-self and flee.

Now the sales teams had departed for other, grander projects, having unloaded all the units, as the saying goes. The unloadees were the usual accountants, doctors, law-yers, and a flock of airline pilots who commuted to Logan. Vine-covered and stalwart, the Birmingham seemed like a respectable address. According to Detective Richard Stein, however, at least two of the units had been acquired by local purveyors of nose candy, who no doubt had a ready-made clientele in affluent next-door neighbors. I mean who but doctors, lawyers, and flyboys can afford a hundred dol-lars a sneeze?

45

As I crossed the slate-and-marble foyer I wondered if Mandy had been one of the retail drug customers. It seemed likely. I had a little trouble with the key and was jiggling the lock when the door flew out of my hands, opening inward.

"And who the fuck," said Bo Bernardi, "are you?"

Having been assured by the Governor that the apartment was empty, I could only gape. Bo Bernardi is not my idea of a hunk, but he looked pretty good with his shirt off. James Dean could have taken sulk lessons from him and learned a few things. Behind him I heard a woman's voice, one I recognized.

"You better let her in, honey," said Kitty O'Hare, who came into the entranceway looking somewhat more disheveled than barechested, barefooted Bo.

The smell of sex was on both of them and if Bo hadn't closed the door behind me I'd have backed on out of there. There was something about a rival sibling sleeping with the supposedly bereaved husband in the recently dead sister's bed that left me a little breathless.

"Hi, Connie." Kitty's eyes told me she knew I knew what they'd just been up to. "You're working for Daddy now, aren't you?"

"What a fucking circus," grumbled Bo. He marched into another room, neatly swiveling his hips to clear a Boston fern that was almost big enough to shade Liechtenstein.

I had been under the impression that Bo and Mandy had not been cohabitating, and mentioned that to Kitty by way of apologizing for my unannounced entrance.

"Nah," she said. "Bo isn't staying here. He has his own place. What we did, was we just sort of decided to drop in and try the place out, you know? I'm thinking maybe I'll buy it from the estate."

"The estate?" For some reason the word boggled me.

"Yeah, you know her will and stuff like that?" said

46

Kitty. The little grin at the end of it reminded me that "stuff like that" amounted to several million.

Our conversation was awkward, though not because Kitty showed any sign of embarrassment. She was a little dazed and I wondered it it was the workout with Bo, or if Dr. Sutcliffe was still poking his needle into her.

"Oh yeah," she said absently. "Bo is taking the stereo. Is that okay with you?"

I looked at her, trying to gauge if the remark was meant to be sarcastic. She seemed amiable enough as she indicated a pile of electronic equipment stacked under the fern.

"Mandy wouldn't have cared," she explained. "But you know how the Alfreds are about things."

"The Alfreds" were her father and grandfather. It was a phrase Mandy had coined and it made me smile.

When Bo came back into he vestibule area he was wearing a fancy western shirt and tooled cowboy boots with big heels that put him in the vicinity of six feet. The sulk had passed from his face, which was now passive and still. The features were handsome enough, I supposed, although his mouth bothered me. The lips were slightly pursed and too weak for his dimpled chin.

"So you're peeping for the lizard," he said. He sat down on one of the big speakers and flicked his fingers over the toes of his cowboy boots. "That's a hell of a job, sweetheart."

Kitty explained that "the lizard" was Bo's term of endearment for Alfred O'Hare, Sr. In a way it was reasonably descriptive, but I tried a look of worldly disapproval. Bo wasn't impressed.

"All I can say, I hope you got paid up front." He looked over at Kitty with spermy eyes and then laughed bitterly. "That old lizard, he hates to part with a shekel. Hell, I know local contractors he's kept in court for years, just sleazing out of paying a bill."

My father had similar, if not more bitter things to say about the Governor, whose penchant for courtroom attachments was almost as strong as his addiction to running for office. Thinking about lawyers and courtrooms reminded me that Bo had more than a passing acquaintance with both. Just to be a nuisance I asked him how he'd made out with the assault charge he'd been picked up for the night Mandy was murdered.

Kitty glowered at me. Bo merely chuckled.

"Shee-it, lady, that was one of my better moves, you know?" He made a little flurry of fists in the air under his own chin. Though not especially large, they were durable-looking fists. "All I did was swear off that asshole who runs the door at the New Dolphin. Never touched a hair on his pointy little head. Thing of it is, I think they pressed charges just to be sociable. Simple assault don't mean shit, so I never even bothered calling my lawyer to post bail. I just hung out with my good buddies down at the cop shop. Hey, ain't my good buddy Detective Stein a good buddy of yours? Like maybe a bosom buddy?"

I laughed right along with him. Bosom is such an odd little word. I wondered if Bo was a bosom man, or if he went in for gams.

"What it was," he was saying, "I was just plain lucky."

I remarked that his was a strange kind of luck.

"You don't get it, do you?" he said, shaking his head. Secret eye signals were still passing between him and Kitty, little blinks that sparked like embers. "Old Mr. Lizard would have had me tried, convicted, and executed by now if he had the tinest little idea I had a hand in what happened to poor little Mandy. As it is he's going to keep his law firm busy making sure I never collect a penny of the dough she left me. Don't think I ain't figured *that* one by now."

Kitty had sidled up next to him and her hands tugged

48

at the collar of his shirt. "Come on, Bo honey," she said with a trace of urgency. "We should get on out of here."

He slipped an arm around her hips and tugged her closer. "Don't you fret now. It don't matter if I run my mouth at this broad. If she works for the lizard she already knows everything bad there is to know about me."

I don't know why I'd expected him to be a little more sensitive about the fact that his wife had been dead for less than a week. Obviously he and Mandy had been married in only the strictest of legal senses. Evidently his indiscretion was infectious, because I said as much.

He was not in the least offended, although I could see Kitty bridling at his side. "Shee-it, you want me to wear a black arm band or something, lady? Would Mandy do that for me? I mean come on, who we talking about here? Don't get the idea I wasn't sort of crazy about the little bitch, 'cause I was. Kitty here knows that. Right, Kitty?"

Kitty was unmoved. I got the distinct impression her big sister was history, and history was a subject that had always bored the pants off her. Of course it didn't take much to get the pants off Kitty, from what I'd heard.

"I don't suppose it's any of my business," I said. "But why did you and Mandy get married in the first place?"

Bo drew himself up to full height, which gave the impression he was twelve or thirteen feet tall. Kitty seemed to shrink beside him and she gave me one very venomous glance that she must have thought better of, because she quickly made it blank and cutsie-pie.

"Well," drawled Bo, "I guess you don't know every dirty little thing about me after all. You want to know why Mandy and I got hitched you better go ask Mr. Lizard O'Hare, ain't that right, Kitty honey?"

"Anything you say," said Kitty doubtfully. She tugged at him again. "You get the speakers, Bo. Connie here will hold the door for us."

When it came to picking up free stereo speakers, Bo was a regular muscleman. I wondered if he and Kitty were going to set up housekeeping somewhere and needed mood music. Whatever their intentions, I was glad to be rid of them and held the door wide, aware that I might very well be aiding and abetting a crime.

There were three Mandy O'Hares in her bedroom. The three became infinite as I glanced into the big double mirrors at her dressing table. Light streamed in through gauze curtains at the window balcony and softened the hard edges of the high-tech interior. The most familiar Mandy was about twelve years old, her corn-silk hair done up in a girlish bob. It was an oil portrait and the artist had managed to touch the spark of her by accenting the mischievous smile and the daring glint in her green-flecked eyes.

The other two Mandys were photographs. The largest, ostentatiously matted and framed, was by a famous society photographer. It was the smaller photograph that intrigued me. It was pinned up with thumb tacks to the cherry facade of a built-in wardrobe. Although the edges were beginning to curl and yellow, the subject matter was as glossy as the day it had been printed. Mandy sitting on a lobstertrap table at her beach cottage, wearing a tank top and denim cutoffs. She had a big can of Australian beer in one hand, a joint in the other, and enough pills inside her to make her smile strangely beatific. In the blurred background a party was in progress.

I had taken the picture myself, given her the snapshot, and forgotten all about it until it jumped at me from her wardrobe. A lucky shot, because it revived that sense of personality I'd been unable to trace anywhere else in the condo unit, the furnishings of which seemed to have been installed by the architects with very little interference from Mandy. The place had all the individuality of a pair of designer jeans and was just about as comfortable.

I wandered down the steps into what is known as a "conversation pit" and found a seat there that looked like it wouldn't swallow me. Bo Bernardi and little sister Kitty had left their spoor on the fluffy rug. I thought about the two of them and tried to decide whether I should report their little escapade to Alfred, also known as "Lizard" to at least one member of the working class. It was a nasty little tidbit, just the thing the old boy was after. And yet who was I to judge their love as true, false, or merely carnal?

I tossed a mental coin, saw it come up tails, and picked up the telephone. Scratch Alfred, he probably knew already. I pressed the playback on Mandy's answering system. I should have been prepared, but the sound of her voice whispering huskily in my ear startled me.

"Hello, hello. This is Mandy but I'm not here or else I'm in one of my moods and not answering the phone. So leave me a message when the little bell rings or try again later . . ."

This was followed by a series of clicks that indicated at least two callers who had not left messages. The one who did was my bosom buddy Bo Bernardi.

Hey Mandy, you really there? Come on answer me if you're on the extension . . . ah fuck, I hate these machines. Look, I want to get together with you immediately. We got something to discuss, if you know what I mean.

There was no dating device on the cassette machine, so I had no way of determining when the call had been made. Mandy was a telephone addict, as witnessed by the dozen extensions in the apartment, so I assumed she cleared her calls at least once a day. Therefore Bo had probably called sometime the day or evening before she went to the motel with Tony Steel.

Husbands called their wives frequently and, much as I hesitated to include Bo in the category, there was no reason why he should not be calling his wife, estranged or not. Still, it made me wonder if he had come to the Birmingham for more than just a quick lay and a free stereo. Had he, perhaps, wanted to check out his call and see if his famous mouth had said anything indiscreet? Or maybe criminal? I kept thinking about the friendly coke salesmen just down the hall, ready and willing to pull out their cute little gram scales at the drop of a c-note. There was the matter of a small vial of white powder that found its way to the Sea Breeze Motel and was now a prime exhibit in the case against Tony Steel. The opposition campaign would not bother connecting Pudge to the fact that his daughter used drugs, but cocaine had a funny way of sticking to politicians who were anywhere in its vicinity. It might be a line of investigation, so to speak, worth pursuing.

The telephone rang. When I got my heart beating again I picked up the receiver. The Governor was speaking to me out of an electronic canyon.

"Yes, sir," I said. "She was here when I entered. I'm not sure, she said something about buying the condo from the estate. That's correct. No, everything seems to be in order. Progress? That will all be in my written report. So far it's been pretty routine. Yes, I remember you saying that, sir, and you can be sure I'll call you if anything remarkable surfaces. Yes, sir, I think I do know what you mean by 'remarkable.' Best to you, too, Governor."

I just couldn't bring myself to call him Alfred. I had a cat once by that name. Unlike the Governor it never used its claws or showed its teeth.

Chapter Eight

In the dream a cricket sat in the corner of my bedroom. The cricket was the size of a small boy. The boy was Alfie and the cricket belonged to him. He had it on a leash and had come to show it to me. Neither of them spoke. They just waited in the corner of my bedroom, watching me sleep. The cricket had eyes as black as onyx and mandibles that glistened in the moonlight.

The cricket began to make a buzzing noise that, in the way of dreams, became the sound of a telephone ringing. I picked up the receiver from the nightstand. The base fell to the floor and bounced under the bed, but the connection did not break. The small miracles of Mother Bell.

"Time for all good little investigators to rise and shine."

I rolled over, burying my head and the receiver in the pillow. Out of the corner of one bleary eye I made sure Alfie and his cricket were gone.

"Richard? What time is it?"

"Four in the morning, sugar pie. Are you conscious yet?"

"No."

"Fine. This is not me calling, do you understand? Maybe you heard about it on the police scanner."

"I don't have a scanner."

"I know. Be hypothetical for once and get your sweet little tush down to the Sea Breeze Motel. The alley behind it. Open your eyes, you're in for a big surprise."

This last was in the singsong of "The Teddy Bears' Picnic," a tune Stein sometimes whistled for hours at a time. Very irritating.

"What's this all about, Richard?"

He told me to come down and find out.

Never mind that the faint glow at the edge of the sky was starting to expand; as far as I was concerned it was still the middle of the night. There are people who pop out of bed, yodel a few bars of something cheerful, and spoon up the Cheerios, grinning at each little ray of dawn. Not me. The best I could do was switch on to servomatic, dress awkwardly, and splash cold water on my face.

I don't remember driving over to the Sea Breeze, but must have done so without incident, because I found myself parked behind Stein's unmarked cruiser. I got out, stomach shaky with a morning nausea that had nothing to do with pregnancy. According to the clock in my body chemistry I was supposed to be safe abed.

Stein's wasn't the only cruiser. There were two others in the lot at the Sea Breeze, as well as a Cadillac with an M.D. shield on the rear license plate. I knew who owned the Caddy and had a pretty good idea of why he was there.

A city garbage truck was blocking the alley. Beyond it I could see a number of people, some in uniform, some not. Turning in I almost tripped over Dr. Nesmith, the county coroner. He was kneeling beside a city worker, a barrel-chested man with a ruddy face that had drained pale. He was slumped against the wall, his gray overalls open at the neck while Nesmith applied a stethoscope to his heart.

"Breathe deep. Again."

I looked the city worker over, wondering if he had been shot; except for a tinge of green about the jowls he looked fine. Evidently Dr. Nesmith agreed with me.

"Okay, Charley. The ticker is ticking along like a good ticker should. Just sit here with your knees up until the dizzy spell passes. When you feel better have someone drive you over to the hospital. Check in with Dr. Treffle or Dr. Burns. They'll probably recommend an EKG, just to be safe."

Nesmith got up and carried his black bag into the alley. I followed, still not completely awake. The narrow gap between buildings seemed to exude a fog of its own, quite different from the mist crawling in over the harbor. The dank, earthy smell of damp brick hovered under the musk of pungent garbage. There was another, sweeter perfume and I fancied that Dr. Nesmith's nose twitched when it touched him.

Portable arc lights were being rigged up and they snapped on as we approached (not that Nesmith ever acknowledged my presence), bleaching the dull brick and making the newly painted dumpster incandescent.

"Make way for Citizen Kale!"

I recognized Detective Sergeant Rosen's somewhat nasal voice and when my eyes adjusted I could see him there. Stein had his back to us and was directing a technician who was positioning the arc lights.

"Hi, Tim."

"Hi, Connie. Jesus, you didn't waste any time."

I told him I'd been listening to the scanner and he laughed. He turned up the collar of his mack and grinned. "I see you brought along your camera, Connie. So how about taking one of me? Believe me, I'm better looking than that thing over there."

"I'll take everyone's picture, Tim. Now what's this all about?"

"You had your breakfast?"

"No."

"Then take a peek."

I leaned around the dumpster unit, which came up to the level of my chest. Something jumped inside me, not because of the dead man, which I'd expected, but because the jiggling arc lights made it look as if he were quivering there, curled up against the wall. The face was turned to the wall and I could see a gold chain cutting into the neck, which was swollen with corruption. One bloated arm was extended toward the dumpster, with fingers like curled sausages.

He looked like something washed up by a storm tide.

"Handsome, ain't he?"

I was not in the mood to trade lines at four in the morning. Sensing this, Tim Rosen decided to leave me alone. After Stein checked in with Dr. Nesmith he came over to me, leaned against the dumpster, and asked for a cigarette.

"I thought you quit?"

"I did. Now I'm unquit again."

When I lit him up a hot piece of the match broke off and burned a hole in my sleeve. The sting almost woke me up.

"Who is it?" I asked.

"Don't know. We want to get pictures before we roll him to check the pockets. Looks like a stab wound, then again it might be gunshot. Pretty crusty."

He was referring to the short-sleeved nylon shirt on the corpse, which was stiff with a dried dark substance I assumed was blood. The arc lights did funny things to color.

"Thanks, Richard. I guess."

He chuckled. "I figure you can keep the Governor off my back."

Stein leaned into me, putting his legs against mine, his

eyes laughing, and whispered that we couldn't keep meeting like this. I agreed. Then he gave me a brief rundown of the find. The city worker had hooked up one of the two cables that lifted the dumpster, walked around to hitch up the other side, and tripped over the corpse. He landed on his back and found himself eye to eye with the dead man, only they weren't really eyes, merely sockets of vermin.

"The guy got spooked pretty bad. His partner thought maybe his heart was going, so Nezzy checked him out. He's okay."

"When do they empty the dumpster? How often?"

Stein shot tendrils of smoke out his nostrils and reinhaled through his lips. For some reason the smoke reminded me of ectoplasm. I waited for an answer, thinking maybe I'd stumped him for once, but he was only playing me along.

"Once a week," he said. "So the last time was a day before Mandy got it. You're pretty sharp, Connie."

"I feel very dull at the moment. You bring a thermos?"

He hadn't, although Detective Rosen was more than willing to share a styrofoam cup of coffee with me. I turned down his offer of a jelly doughnut. Somehow it didn't seem appropriate. Rosen left me alone with the last few swallows of cooling coffee and I sipped it, coming into full consciousness as I watched the men work.

Ground was chalked. Tape measures were snapped. A photographer (apparently new to the department, since I didn't recognize her) exposed several rolls of film. I took a few shots of my own because I'd found that clients appreciate seeing a file spruced up with photographs. The investigator had to look at this ugly corpse, the file says, that's why her bill is so outrageous.

When the scene had been recorded from every conceivable angle, Dr. Nesmith was let into the chalked area. He knelt beside the corpse and began to prod it gently. I was impressed by how methodical and matter-of-fact the police procedure was. As small as Rivermuth is in the scheme of things, we have our share of homicides. But of the twenty or so that happen in a year, virtually all are of the estranged-husband-shoots-wife variety, sometimes vice versa. Even what happened to Mandy was not really far afield, since the "boyfriend" (albeit a sudden one) had been taken into custody and charged with the crime. The corpse in the alley would no doubt turn out to be the victim of robbery. The last time it had happened, a local cab driver was found slumped over his wheel, shot dead, and robbed. Detective Stein had pulled the rabbit out of the hat by arresting a merchant sailor who was dumb enough to leave the murder weapon in his seabag. It was a nice piece of work. That was how I'd first gotten to know Richard, when he yanked the rug out from under me before I had a chance to impress the cab driver's family with my investigative acumen.

Now I watched curiously as he pulled on a pair of rubber gloves and helped Nesmith turn the body over. Both men began to gag and then the miasma hit me, too. Gas escaping from the frail vessel of flesh. I was glad I'd refused the pastry. After a few minutes the odor dispersed somewhat and they grimly returned to the task. Because of the swelling the pants and shirt were skin tight, already starting to give at the seams. Nesmith used a scalpel to cut away a pocket and then gingerly extracted a wallet.

Stein held the wallet in his rubber gloves. He had the lab technician dust for prints right there, on a portable lab table. I knew from the expression on his face that he didn't expect to get any. When the tech shook his head Stein pulled off the gloves and flipped the wallet open with the stub of a pencil. Even from where I was the thick wedge of green bills was visible.

So much for robbery. I remember being rather surprised that Stein didn't seem to be the least bit disappointed.

"What's the prelim, Doc?" he asked Nesmith, who was still attending the corpse.

"Lividity has come and gone," said the coroner. "Same with rigor. From the intestinal distension I'd say decay is fairly advanced, at least three days in this weather. As many as five."

Mandy had been dead four days. Stein had the wallet fully open now and he and Rosen were gently examining several small, plastic credit cards. No one was paying much attention to me and I sidled closer. When Rosen turned over the last card he whistled.

"Bingo," he said. "The late Jon Maxfield."

"God damn," said Richard softly. "God damn."

The name meant nothing at first. After a few moments it clicked in place. Jon "Maximum Jon" Maxfield, one-time cellmate and later a professional associate of Anthony "Tony Steel" Alamia, presently occupying a solo cell in the basement of the Rivermuth Police Station.

I had not noticed the advent of daylight. Suddenly there it was, seeping over the brick walls, washed out and no match yet for the arc lights. I could feel the air moving and knew the tide changed. Gulls were complaining about breakfast over the harbor. All things considered it was going to be a fine morning.

There was an eerie, not unpleasant sense of time slowing to a stop. I wanted the feeling to last, not because I liked being in a garbage-strewn alley with a corpse, but because for a few moments I had once again fallen in love with the profession I'd stumbled into by accident. There are times, lots of them, when the tedium of investigation convinces me that my second career is as big a mistake as my first had been. It's not the poking into other peoples' lives and deaths that makes it good, it's the *being there* when something happens.

Feelings like that never last long, and when the sense

of temporal suspension melted away I was left with the burnt taste of bad coffee and a belly that had begun to protest an emptiness that was anything but existential. I had decided to leave, having seen enough of the late Jon Maxfield, when Dr. Nesmith made the discovery.

"Dick? I have something here."

Stein muttered what might have been a mild prayer. He gave me one of his this-is-it looks and ambled over to where Nesmith squatted, scalpel in hand. I could hear the sound of fabric tearing—I hoped it was fabric—and then Nesmith grunted and held up a small plastic bundle.

The bundle was a zip-lock baggie. Richard took it from the coroner, weighed it in the palm of his hand, and unraveled the plastic. I could see the caked white powder. Richard dabbed his forefinger into this and rubbed a little of what stuck across the front of his gums, under his upper lip. Nobody spoke. Then Tim Rosen did a little victory jig and I got the impression he had just won a bet with Detective Richard Stein.

Richard was not amused. He handed the plastic bag to the lab technician and spit into the dumpster, rinsing out his mouth with a partial cup of cooled coffee.

"I got a funny feeling about this," he said to his partner Rosen. "Do you have a funny feeling, Timothy?"

Rosen was absolutely gleeful. "Oh yes," he said. "A very funny feeling."

Me, too. And no one would tell me what the hell was going on.

Chapter Nine

The servile voice on the other end of the line informed me cordially that he was not in fact one of the domestics, but merely a student of Hippocrates.

"Pardon me, Dr. Sutcliffe." I apologized. "I didn't expect to get you there at five in the morning."

"The children, you know," he murmured, having forgotten to amend it to the singular, since Kitty was now the last of the O'Hare progeny. "And Pudge has a touch of the flu. It's exhausting work, running for Congress. One must come into physical contact with all sorts of less than hygienic people."

After a momentary hesitation I decided to take him literally. If he had suddenly developed a sense of humor I didn't want to deal with it at that hour of the morning. When the Governor came on the line his voice was husky and full; if I had awakened him he made no complaint.

"Fill me in," he said.

I filled him in. When I was done he sighed, cleared his throat, and said in a weary voice, "Sounds rather like some kind of orgy, doesn't it? Sex and drugs and murder. Very familiar connection, these days."

I said it was too soon to speculate. It did seem probable that Tony Steel would be charged with an additional murder. How exactly Jon Maxfield fit into the picture on the night in question was still very much up in the air.

"That isn't what I meant at all," he said. "I mean the other side will use it against us, one way or another. We have one dead girl and two male prostitutes, one of them in jail and the other murdered a few yards from where the girl was found. The rumormongers will say 'orgy' or more probably they will say 'drug-crazed sex orgy' or something along that line. So you see, Connie, the truth has very little bearing here."

I mumbled an apology. He cut me short.

"Oh never mind that. I can't be expecting you to develop an instant expertise on public relations. There are others paid quite handsomely to do that." It was interesting to hear him change gears so adroitly. I could feel my ears warming as he burbled with his idea of gruff charm. "Providing this sort of information before the media steps all over it is exactly what *you* were hired to do. So rather than being a grumpy old grandpa who hasn't had enough beauty sleep I should be congratulating you on doing a fine job."

The early slant of daylight was stealing across my kitchen floor, showing up tumbleweeds of dust. I looked up at the ceiling where the cobwebs were no less visible. One of these days I'd have to find a broom, or move out.

"Things are looking up," the Governor was saying chattily. It was an unworthy thought, but I wondered if Sutcliffe had given him a morning booster. "The latest polls came in last night. Pudge gained eight points over the last showing. We're going to increase the television saturation."

When the conversation concluded he sounded satisfied. If the old man thought I had helped, I wasn't about to correct him. I managed to filter a pot of coffee without spilling the water and took it out to the sunporch, where the dew on the windows sparkled with the morning light.

"Salud!"

I thought maybe one of Jesus Christ's avocado arms would wave back when I saluted her with my coffee mug. At most there was a dry rustle of her three yellowing leaves. I settled into the wicker rocker with the Tony Steel file in my lap. My head had cleared enough to begin formulating a schedule for the day. The county coroner was due to begin the Maxfield autopsy at two in the afternoon, which left me a good many hours to spare. With that in mind I began to collate the transcript references to the late Jon Maxfield.

> STEIN: Okay, Tony. Let's get back to your friend Maxfield. If I have it right you and he got acquainted in Thomaston and when you got out he arranged for you to go to work doing this, ah, thing you do.
> STEEL: Yeah. It was really this guy Arnold Maury, Maxie knew him from before he went in. Like I said, the guy owns the Ranchero, which is like this big lounge in Portland. Also he's a booking agent for rock bands and wrestlers and these specialty acts like what Max and Randy and me do.
> STEIN: Is this Arnold Maury a loan shark by any chance?
> STEEL: I wouldn't know nothing about that.

As I sifted through the pages it became obvious that Richard had a sincere interest in Mr. Maury and Mr. Maxfield and their relationship to Mr. Steel. What exactly that interest was had not been included in the file I'd duped in his office.

STEEL: Like I said before, Maxie wasn't what you'd call reliable. So it wasn't the first time he was a no-show for a gig. Randy was all bent out of shape about it but personally I didn't care. We hustle a little, we make more on tips, that's my philosophy.

STEIN: You say Randy was bent out of shape. Is he as friendly with Maxfield as you are?

STEEL: You kidding? Maxie hates faggots. Me, I could care less, but Max has this thing about it and he likes to give Randy a hard time.

STEIN: I'd like to have a few words with Jon Maxfield. You have any idea how I can get a hold of him?

STEEL: Hey, doan worry. Once he hears I'm in trouble he'll come in. Maxie will turn up eventually.

Tony Steel was right about that. If he had been the one who killed Jon Maxfield I had to admire his nerve while under interrogation. He couldn't possibly be as simple as the transcripts made him sound. No one could be.

It was so pleasant on the sunporch that I had to use the forward motion of the rocking chair to overcome my inertia. Once I was up and ambling I decided to voyage east to Portland and see a man about a stripper.

The lobby was paved with plastic grass that skittered under my plimsolls. The walls leading to the inside entrance were papered with publicity shots preserved under sheets of Plexiglas. The photographs seemed to be arranged in crude chronology. The older shots were of beefy men in high-waisted wrestling trunks, posing over names like Mister Fat Boy, the Assassin, Big Bobby True, and Doctor Nervo. The man called Nervo was holding a large black doctor bag in one meaty hand and displaying a

64

stethoscope in the other. You got the impression he might use the stethoscope to strangle his opponents.

As I drifted toward the inner door I stopped to glance at a stripper who called herself Wonder Woman. Wonder Woman was a sultry girl of forty or so, wearing a torn bikini bottom and what had to be a pair of cruelly siliconized breasts. The more recent male strippers were in a separate frame of Plexiglas near the door. No one had bothered to remove the autographed glossy of Mr. Maximum. Possibly the management had not yet been apprised of his recent departure from the stage of life. I was rather hoping they hadn't.

The interior of the Ranchero Lounge and Dance was barn-sized and so dimly lit I staggered, tripped up by the transition from plastic grass to waxed linoleum.

"Hang on, lady," said a voice in the distance. "You stay put and I'll hit the dimmer."

I swayed, hands outstretched, and waited until the bar lights came up. In the cavernous distance a horseshoe-shaped bar was now softly illuminated and I could see well enough to navigate across the fifty yards or so of empty dance floor.

"At night it ain't so bad, dear," said the man inside the horseshoe. "But coming in out of the bright sun, heck it's like getting poleaxed, ain't it?"

I agreed. I was trying not to stare open mouthed at Doctor Nervo. The spitcurl beard had gone gray and he was wearing custom-built overalls instead of gym trunks, but he would have been recognizable even without the huge chromed championship buckle that just managed to span his remarkable diameter.

"Whatsamatter, lady," said Nervo in his thin, high inflected voice. "Ain't you never seen a four-hundred-pound bartender?"

I took a swivel seat, placed the manila file on the bar, and said, "As a matter of fact, no."

"Well shucks all over me, lady." Nervo spun on his relatively small feet, displaying his unseen portions. I felt like a satellite tracking the backside of the moon. "You know how many square feet of orange poplin they is in these overalls? Why it's no less than three hundred and sixty two, that's how many. That is six feet even from shoulder to toe and the same around the waist. Fella in here the other night tole me I looked like the biggest, meanest tangerine in the world."

"You are," I said, "an extremely large man."

"You're no midget yourself, lady, heightwise." A fore-finger the size of California on a large map poked at the corner of the manila file. "You a salesman? Excuse me, sales*lady?* 'Cause if you from the Budweiser people I just wanna warn you I'm about to pour myself a great big pitcher of Pabst Blue Ribbon, which is my breakfast."

I denied any affiliation with the Budweiser people. A bottle of Pabst was uncapped and placed before me, along with a glass. I did not think it was opportune to remark on the early hour. I definitely wanted Doctor Nervo to be my friend.

"They make that Bud stuff over in Merrimack, New Hampshire, lady. You can drive on over there anytime and go in that new plant and drink yourself sick if you want."

"No thanks. Pabst Blue Ribbon, that's the stuff." I took a sip from the glass to prove it. While not my idea of breakfast, it was an improvement on soggy Wheaties.

"Personally my feeling for Pabst is on account of my mum, God rest her. Lady, that little ole gal sure loved her beer. She wasn't near as big as me, but she was what they call obese, in a small sort of way."

"God bless the small and obese," I said genially.

"What Mum was, she was short and real fat. Now take me, I got lots of muscle tissue just holding me up, but Ma lacked that and so we had her fixed in a chair. Not your normal little wheelchair because they don't come that wide.

66

A regular chair it was, that me and my brother Fred built wheels on so Ma could get to the fridge."

I had decided I was being set up for a tall—or rather fat—tale. Nevertheless I did not risk a smile because Doctor Nervo looked serious enough under his beard.

"Lady, my mum really appreciated that special chair we give her. The kitchen floor kind of sagged a little toward the middle from the strain, and Ma, she'd coast right on down and wheel her up smart. We fixed this shelf, see, under the chair seat, just big enough to hold a case of quarts. Me and Fred was going to put a little cooler under there but she passed away on us."

"I'm sorry to hear that," I said.

Doctor Nervo laughed, holding one hand over the chromed championship buckle. "Lady, I appreciate how hard you're trying to believe my lies."

"Oh really?"

"Heck yes. Ma weren't no Pabst fiend. She drunk herself to death on Pickwick Ale."

Nervo told me the Ranchero wasn't officially open until noon. The lobby door had been unlocked because the beer reps were accustomed to calling on Wednesday morning. Nervo said he was the head bartender and owned what he described as a "light-weight" share of the operation.

"Just enough to keep me honest," he said, slicing cardboard tops off beer cases with a pearl-handled switchblade. "I used to be what they called a liar and a cheater in the ring, lady. So Mr. Arnold put me on shares to keep my itsy bitsy fingers out of the till."

"You threw fights?"

"Threw *fights?* Heck no, lady. I never lost a fight in my life. Ta *other* guy mighta thrown 'em, maybe, but not Doctor Nervo. I had me three thousand two hunret and forty-six professional engagements an' I won every single one by unanimous enthusiasm and superior density. What I did was, sometimes I used what they call an illegal hold. The

'Bear Claw' for instance. And I had me a specialized 'Super Python' that was foolproof.''

"A 'Super Python,'" I said. "Sure wish I'd seen you put *that* on somebody."

A big mistake. One moment I was sitting there calmly, adjusting the head of beer in the pilsner glass; the next thing I knew I was being liften upside down, my hair hanging down toward the bartop and the rest of my body floating somewhere above. I kicked my legs feebly as enormous hands held me. The blood rushed into my head, putting a pink mist over everything. Doctor Nervo grunted, the world turned right side up, and I was back in my seat again.

"Jesus." I said. "*Christ.*"

"One heck of a hold, ain't she?" Nervo's cheeks were rosy and he was panting. "Lady, I must be getting old. Took the air out of me, putting a 'Python' on a little shrimp like you."

"Me?" I was flattered. As the tallest girl in my high school class I'd been categorized as a lummox. "A shrimp?"

"Relatively speakin'. I once put her on Big Bobby True and he had a density in the neighborhood of four hunret pounds. Then I went and let him slip and he tore a hole right through the canvas, which came out of my share of the gate. Always figured Bobby shoulda paid. It was his pointy head ripped it."

I sipped at the beer and listened, careful not to admire any more of the wrestling holds he mentioned. The pink mist cleared from my head and I was ready to believe that my temporary suspension had been imagined—how *had* he reached over the bar? I found I was rather liking the taste of Pabst as a substitute for brunch. On the drive north to Portland I'd been thinking about trying on a story. After meeting Doctor Nervo I decided maybe the truth, or part of it, would be a better place to start.

When he had finished with the beer cases and put away

the pearl-handled knife, I said, "When you get a chance, I've got a couple of young ladies I'd like you to look over."

"That sounds nice," he laughed in his little voice. "I like girls."

I slid the photographs out of the manila folder and handed them over. Nervo held them carefully by the edges and studied them. "Very pretty. These sisters of yours?"

"Not exactly. Just friends."

"Friends, huh?" He sounded doubtful. "But the drift is, has Doctor Nervo seen 'em? Is that the drift?"

"That's the drift," I admitted.

He handed the snapshots back and I propped them up against my glass.

"Lady, it's this way. They is a whole lot of girls come in here. Come over from Berwick and Ellsworth and as far away as Caribou, on a warm night."

"I appreciate that."

"Who you want to ask is Mr. Arnold Maury. He's what they call the principal owner here." He said this softly, looming close enough for me to smell the Pabst on his breath. "What it is, lady, it ain't for me to say if I saw someone or not."

When Doctor Nervo came around the corner of the horseshoe I backed up instinctively, suspecting I was about to be thrown out, possibly in a very literal way.

"So," said Nervo, with what might have been a wink. "You wanna ask Mr. Maury?"

"Sure," I said uneasily. "How do I do that?"

How I did it was to follow the giant bartender through a partial circumference of the big room and out a rear exit. The exit opened into a small parking lot. A cold spot in my belly expanded into a lump of ice, because I knew that if Nervo had something physical in mind the deserted parking lot was the perfect place for it. I know a little basic karate but it wouldn't have worked on a professional wrestler who was only slightly smaller than the second moon of Jupiter. Not to worry. He merely led me politely into an adjacent building.

Nervo took a key from his belt and unlocked the door, which led into a partitioned hallway, bare except for a blood-red carpet. At the end of the runner was an open office door. Nervo tapped his knuckles on the casing and said, with gentle deference, "A lady of distinction to see you, Mr. Maury."

The wrestler backed away, leaving me in an L-shaped office. It was furnished in matching blond oak, high quality stuff I wouldn't mind having in my own office, if I ever bother setting one up. The Oriental on the floor looked genuine, as did the crystal vase of fresh-cut flowers. It was not what I had expected after seeing the Ranchero Lounge, nor was the slender man on the telephone old enough to be the cigar-chomping booking agent I had pictured in my mind.

There were no cigars in evidence, not even an ashtray. I estimated Arnold Maury at no more than thirty-five and modishly attired enough to be a criminal lawyer rather than a booker of male strippers and mud-wrestling girls. He was speaking into a shielded phone that covered his mouth. I did catch a glimpse of the small gold stud in his left ear-lobe, which seemed in odd contrast to his precisely styled hair and the narrow pinstripe that I guessed might be off-the-rack from Louis of Boston.

His small gray eyes stripped off my coat and blouse and were peeling off my pants when I sat down abruptly on one of the Naugahyde settees. That was when I noticed the long, clear lacquered nail on the little finger on his right hand. He returned the telephone to the cradle and grinned at me.

"What can I do for you, Miss Body Beautiful? The fat man hires the cocktail waitresses, so you must want something special, huh?"

"That's it exactly," I said. What I wanted to do was remove that lacquered fingernail and scratch it in his eyes. Instead I slipped the snapshots out of the folder and put them on the desk blotter. "What I'm doing here, Arnold, is I'm trying to determine if either of these women ever frequented your establishment."

The leopard smile slowly dissolved. Maury leaned forward, his fingertips meeting in an attitude of prayer. "Mmmm," he said. "Is that so? Two very attractive young ladies. But then I see many attractive women in the course of a day, Miss . . . ah?"

"Kale." I said. "Connie Kale."

"Is that so? That's a real nice name, Miss Kale. Would you like a drink or something? I can buzz for it."

"No, thank you. There's no need to buzz for anything."

Arnold Maury studied his nails and then leveled his eyes at me. It was a maneuver he'd practiced and he did it reasonably well. "I'm not sure what I detect here, dear. You give off this distinct vibration. I get this feeling you are some kind of *busybody*. A do-gooder, am I right?"

"That's one way of looking at it," I said. "I like to think of myself as an investigator. Whether I do any good, is not for me to say."

"An investigator, huh?" He thought that over, shifting the little gray orbs away. "You make a living at this kind of thing, Miss Kale?"

"As a matter of fact I do."

"Yeah? That's real interesting." He leaned back in his padded chair and swiveled, showing me his profile. He was about as cute as a pet tarantula. On the fabric wall behind the blond desk I noticed some of the same publicity stills I'd seen in the lobby, only these were matted and framed in brushed aluminum. Neither Jon Maxfield nor Tony Steel was in evidence. "Can I ask you a question, Miss Investigator?" he asked. "Who exactly are these two girls supposed to be?"

"The blonde one is, or rather was, Mandy O'Hare. The brunette is her younger sister Kitty."

"And you think I know who they are?"

"Sure I do," I said. "I know you know who Mandy O'Hare is. You look like a guy who can watch television, even if you might have a little trouble with a newspaper."

Arnold thought that was pretty funny. At least I think the snorting sound was meant to be laughter. "You got a cute mouth, honey. I like a girl who talks back."

"What I'm trying to determine, Arnold, is if either of the O'Hare sisters ever kept company with Jon Maxfield or Tony Steel."

He considered that for a while. Then he picked up the two snapshots, shuffled one over the other, and handed them back to me.

"You're just full of cute tricks, honey," he said. He was back in control of the leopard smile. "Look, I'll be honest with you. I don't know if Tony killed that little broad or not. Or why you're trying to make Jonny Max fit into it. What you got, some kind of theory? Some story Tony made up?"

"No story, Arnold. I just want to know if either of the O'Hare girls dated either one of your, ah, 'clients' before Mandy was killed. I don't think that's asking a lot of you."

His expression let me know how wrong I was.

"Sweetheart, I am not in the habit of answering questions put to me by wise-ass broads I never heard of. But I'm a square and fair guy, so let me go this far. I don't know if those two chicks ever came into the Ranch or not. We get three or four hundred through the door every night, more on weekends."

I stood up and turned to leave. Maury remained at his desk, looking me over.

"Look, you mind I use a little strong language? Maybe

those two kids were in here every damn night. I got no idea. Maybe they were both screwing Jonny Max, or Tony Steel, or maybe all four of them ganged up to fuck rogue elephants. So you can put any kind of story together, it makes no difference to me. That dumb wop Tony is back in jail where he belongs. And Jonny Max is fired just as soon as he sets foot in here again."

"That might be a long wait."

His eyes narrowed. "Now wait a minute. You know something I should know?"

"I only know what *I* know, Arnold. Not what *you* know."

"Come on. What happened to Maxie?"

I flashed him my imitation of his imitation leopard smile, picked up the manila folder, and headed for the door.

"The cops have him," I said half truthfully. "He's spilling his guts right about now."

As I left the color was draining from Arnold Maury's face.

Chapter Ten

"Take a look at *this* piece of equipment," I heard the coroner say. "A waste of good meat, yes?"

I was in the hospital basement, outside the single room that served as the pathology department. I was sitting in a molded plastic chair of the type designed to nest in stacks. Maybe it had been engineered with birds in mind, because my fairly narrow bottom seemed to overlap all four edges. I'd been there for an hour, lighting cigarettes one end from the other, using them like joss sticks against the stink of formaldehyde.

Richard Stein called jovially from inside. "Hey, Connie. Come in here and see what you're missing."

"Ha ha," said I.

I'd once voluntarily observed the first three or four minutes of an autopsy in the same room. Prior to that I had been to many wakes and seen the usual corpses (including my mother's) displayed like waxen fruit on mock velvet. So it wasn't the dead body laid out on the irrigated marble slab that bothered me. It was what followed. The rapid reduction of a human being, the cutting up and putting into glass jars as each organ is fingered and probed and labeled for mortal fault in indelible coroner's ink. And when they are done there is nothing of interest left, just a hollow husk of bone and skin and vials of things you might find in a nightmare deli counter.

No thanks. I wanted to know what they found in Jon Maxfield, but I wasn't interested in making a visual assessment. Tim Rosen came out of the room, ostensibly to bum a smoke. Lighting him up I noticed he was distinctly green about the gills.

"That Nesmith," he sighed, adding in a lower voice. "He got him a peculiar kind of humor."

"He got him a peculiar kind of job."

Falling into the rhythm of Detective Rosen's southern locution had not been intentional; he gave me a look that said he had matriculated at the University of Virginia and didn't like lending out his speech patterns to Yankee ladies. I smiled an apology just as Richard Stein appeared in the door, his complexion comparatively rosy.

"Look at what the doc turned up."

He opened the palm of his hand. I saw a small particle of metal no bigger than a drop of blood.

"Knife point?" said Tim Rosen.

Stein nodded. "We'll have to wait for the microcomp, but my hunch is that it matches." He looked sideways at me. "Whadaya think of that, Intrepid Investigator?"

"Gumshoe to you," I said. It was easy enough to banter at an autopsy when you didn't actually have to watch Dr. Nesmith wielding his stainless-steel cutting shears. "Maybe," I added, "our Mr. Maximum was a sword swallower, in addition to his other talents."

That got a laugh out of both of them. "Mr. Maximum," said Richard. "Where do they come up with these names?" He cupped his palm and slipped the tiny metal chip into a plastic vial. "Things get curiouser and curiouser, eh, Timothy?"

"Indeed."

"I'm going to take a wild guess," I said. "If the micro-comp is positive then Maxfield and Mandy were killed with the same weapon. I don't suppose you can tell who got it first? With the knife, I mean."

Stein made a moue, widening his dark, heavy-lashed eyes.

"Oh wouldn't *that* be nice to know," he said, using his courtroom voice. "But negatory, Ms. Kale. We poor witless flatfoots must assume, until some expert witness with rattling adenoids disabuses us of the notion, that Mr. Maxfield and, ah, Mrs. Bernardi died by insertion of the same knife in places vital, probably within hours of each other. Possibly minutes. But as to determining who died first, that will be dependent on other factors."

"Other factors? What other factors? Come on, guys, what are you holding back? You *are* assuming Tony Steel killed both of them, right?"

"Well . . ." drawled Stein, giving Rosen a loaded glance. "That is a working hypothesis, eh, Timothy?"

"One of several," agreed Rosen.

"Don't be so bloody mysterious, you two oafs. What have you got, another suspect?"

Richard was already shaking his head. "Oaf that I am, I confess that Anthony is our only suspect. At the moment."

"At the moment? Come on guys, give."

A clearly discernible smirk beamed from Richard's face. "Timothy, I think the young lady wants us to give her information she can auction directly to that elderly states-man affectionately referred to as 'The Governor.'"

"I must say I agree," said Rosen, falling right into the stand-up comic routine.

I had to wince. A quick perusal of the morning papers would give the uninformed reader the information that the body of a twenty-eight-year-old male, dead of undetermined causes, had been discovered at an address on Front Street. There was no mention of a connection to the O'Hare murder, which proved to me once and for all that Alfred O'Hare still had some leverage and was obviously willing to use it. From the flak I was getting, it seemed a safe bet that a good deal of that leverage had been applied to Detectives Stein and Rosen.

"Okay, okay," I said, backing off. "So my client has a bias against the media."

"You might say that," grinned Stein.

"Last I heard both of you gentlemen were similarly inclined," I said. "As a matter of fact I can remember lending a sympathetic ear while you both went on and on about how Truman Hawkins goofed up a case by printing certain facts you wanted withheld . . ."

Mumbled and grumbles.

"She's got a point," said Rosen. "I think it's right on top of her head."

"Lewis and Martin," I said. "Burns and Allen. And now Rosen and Stein."

Richard pulled a face. I don't think he was really irritated. He was a pretty good string-puller himself when he got the chance. I could see him mulling something over and I shut up, hoping it would work out in my favor.

"Okay, Connie. On the who-croaked-first question, we're waiting for Nezzy on that. It's a blood type problem. But there is one interesting little item that came back before we went into Path. Care to take a guess?"

"I'm a lousy guesser. You tell me, oh wise and witty detective."

"Ever hear of mannitol?"

"Baby laxative," I said. "Also used to cut powder-type drugs."

Tim Rosen, who was more of a gentleman than Stein would ever be, had the courtesy to look pleased when I got it right.

"The kid is on the ball," he said. "She may get a merit badge on this one."

"On the beam, Con," said Stein grudgingly. "The cocaine on Maxfield's body was forty-six percent mannitol, twelve percent procaine, thirty-nine percent cocaine, three percent trace. And just by coincidence the stuff we found in the room where Mandy died was—"

"Forty-six percent mannitol, twelve percent procaine, etcetera, etcetera. In other words it was the same stuff. Tony Steel was dealing."

Richard had his hands up and his eyes had that mixed beam of amusement and dead seriousness that had first attracted me to him. "Good so far. But go no further. All we know is that *someone* was dealing. Not who. Could have been any one of the three involved. You like Tony Steel for it? Okay, but Tim and I are reserving judgment."

I was pondering that when a voice close up behind made me jump. "You grow ever more lovely, my dear."

It was foolish to let Dr. Nesmith unnerve me. I had a pretty good idea where the hand he wrapped around my waist had been recently, and it made butterflies boil up inside me.

"Isn't she lovely, Richard?" said the coroner, murmuring more to me than to the others. "I have a thing about tall women. The idea of legs."

I managed to squirm out of his grasp without actually taking hold of those cool, papery hands.

"How about the idea of blood types, Doc?"

Nesmith's spectacles glinted. When he smiled his thin lips disappeared. "All in good time, boys."

Stein and Rosen were still playing their little game of eyelid semaphore, including me out. I decided to pick up my ball and go home. Richard caught up with me in the parking lot and walked me to my car. We walked close enough to touch if either of us had been so inclined. Apparently neither of us was.

"Dinner? My treat."

"Depends," I said. "Will you be explaining all this mystery about blood types and why you're suddenly shy on Tony Steel?"

He shrugged. "Just dinner, Connie. You know how it is."

"Sure I do," I said, unlocking the car door and slipping inside. I rolled down the window. The only explanation for what I said next is that hunger brings out the bitch in me. "Speaking of how it is, how is Anne?"

Watching Richard walk away from me was not an entirely unpleasant experience. Nice buns, for a cop.

Chapter Eleven

There was a surprise waiting on my front porch. I couldn't pull into the driveway because a dark blue Mercedes limousine was blocking the way. Behind the tinted windows I could just make out the profile of a uniformed chauffeur. The vanity plates said OH-10, so I was able to narrow the possibilities down to two.

Pudge O'Hare, Republican candidate for Congress, had a little trouble getting up from the porch swing to greet me. The reason he had trouble standing was because he was extremely drunk.

"Please forgive me," he said.

I thought he was going to cry and I fumbled the keys, in a hurry to open the door and get him inside.

"I'm afraid," he said, "I have been drinking."

Drunk or not he was still meticulously groomed and his suit was unwrinkled. Probably had a valet to look out for him. That's all the average gutter wino needs to keep up appearances—a valet and a few odd million for steam baths and single malt scotch.

The face that looked so unmarked in photographs and

on the television screen had been ravaged of late. Pudge looked as if he had been in a fist fight, possibly with himself. He had sprouted new pouches under his eyes and his skin was the color of tapioca. Whatever color his eyes had once been, they were now mostly red and moistened with the kind of self pity you buy by the quart.

"Very weak of me," he said, responding to my unspoken thoughts. "Not a drinker, you know. Never have been. Not since 'Lisha went in the bin."

Elisha was his wife. Booze had been just one of her many problems and I remembered that Pudge, never a heavy tippler, had given it up entirely when his wife was permanently committed. It was such a happy-go-lucky family, why should anyone need to drink?

I suggested he sit at the kitchen table while I heated up a pot of the coffee brewed early that morning. It wasn't the New Orleans blend he was used to, but I didn't think he'd notice.

"I remember," he told me earnestly, "you and little Mandy. The kingdom in the cupboards."

Oh, I'm rough and tough but a weeping man does it to me every time. I turned away, playing with the coffee, as the memory flooded back. The kingdom in the cupboards. I was seven or eight years old. My father, to keep me out of mother's hair, let me follow him around the Sankaty Head course while he attended to his duties. That's where Mandy and I got thrown together, down at the club house. She was a little hellraiser even then, willful and mischievous, and I followed her lead, helping her to let air out of Cadillac tires (only that model, for some reason), cutting the net lines at the tennis courts, and tipping paint cans into the swimming pool.

Naturally enough I had followed her home. I like to think now that Mandy didn't coax me like a stray dog, although it may have been a little like that. I do remember being very aware that on some level my father was subservient to hers, even more so to her grandfather, that white and fearsome man who owned the golf course and most of the homes surrounding it, which was all the world I knew.

"A sweet little girl," said the candidate dreamily. He ignored the scorched coffee.

The sweet little girl had, at seven years of age, a complete run of the estate at Sankaty Head. While her mother stayed behind the locked doors of her ground floor suite attended by a nurse, Mandy talked back to her governess, a lovely woman by the name of Beatrice, and took great delight in telling the Japanese gardener to "go spit, slant eye!," which was pretty heady stuff for girls of seven. She was never punished or reprimanded; looking back, I doubt that would have had a discernible effect on her behavior. The Governor, a large, frightening figure who in those days seemed always to be wearing elastic swim trunks and floppy sandals, did his best to encourage her outrageousness. I can remember that he had Mandy roll out the brass dumbbells with which he exercised, and he showed her how to make a muscle and a fist for punching, which she immediately tried out on her brother Alfie. The Governor thought her "go spit, slant eye" line was amusing and for years repeated it to company and for all I know to the Japanese gardener himself.

"A princess," Pudge was saying, more to himself than to me.

It was true that there was more to Mandy than pranks and naughtiness. What Pudge was referring to was the secret club we had made in the big pantry in the main house at Sankaty Head. Mandy pulled boards loose under the wainscotting, lit the cubbyhole with a tapered candle stolen from the chapel, and swore Alfie and Kitty and me to secrecy. Mandy was the self-appointed Queen of Augustine (where she got that I never knew—maybe she connected it with the month of August, when she was born). Kitty and I were her Ladies in Waiting and poor Alfie was a mere Vassal, though he didn't mind so long as he was included in the game. The kingdom was active for several years; in the end we played rock'n'roll records in the secret cubbyhole (one of the few things forbidden by Pudge because the noise disturbed Mandy's mother), until we had grown so large we had trouble slipping through the boards. I distinctly remember Mandy smoking a cigarette there to celebrate her eleventh birthday. Smoking it quite successfully, too, in her wanton style.

"I'm not supposed to be here," Pudge told me. "Supposed to be in bed with the flu."

I gathered that the "flu" Dr. Sutcliffe had mentioned was entirely self-administered. And I could understand why his people did not want Pudge out and about in his present condition. I had no idea what he wanted and hesitated to ask. Maybe he wanted me to put on a pasteboard crown and play Queen for a Day with him. Looking at the anguish in his expression made me want to break out a new bottle of Scotch. Instead I pretended to sip the coffee and hoped he would follow my example.

"You didn't hate her," Pudge told me earnestly. He was struggling with something. I'm not sure he knew exactly what. "There was nothing really bad about Mandy. I mean not *really* bad."

I told him I agreed. I told him a lot of things I didn't fully believe. They were things he wanted to hear about his daughter, whose faults he had always overlooked. Although he couldn't bring himself to state it plainly, I finally realized that what had gotten Pudge out of bed was the rumor that Mandy's death had been the result of an orgy. I wondered if he had been on the line when I spoke to his father early that morning. However he had come by it, plainly the image was torturing him and he wanted me to exorcise it by telling him it was not true.

I was happy to oblige. I talked about moonlight and romance and holding hands, laying it on pretty thick. By the time I was done Mandy was still a virgin looking for a magic unicorn and I had half convinced myself of her essential beatitude. Without touching a drop I felt drunker than Pudge, who was starting to sober up.

We were making real progress when Dr. Sutcliffe arrived with the shock troops.

"You had us all in a tizzy," said Sutcliffe. I was a little miffed that he had entered without knocking.

"We're having coffee, are we?" he said to me with a semblance of a smile. "That was very dear of you, Constance. But I do wish you had telephoned."

"The man is fifty-two years old," I said. "He's running for Congress."

"Exactly," said the good doctor. "The poor man has been under tremendous pressure."

Pudge didn't seem to mind being talked about in the third person. I had a sudden intuition that it had always been that way.

"I'm feeling much better," he told Sutcliffe. "This is just what I needed. A little chat with a friend of Mandy's."

"Oh? And what were we chatting about?"

"The kingdom," I said. "The one in the cupboard."

I was glad to see that Sutcliffe was uninitiated. He merely frowned at me and waited while Pudge got to his feet. Two burly young men in button-down collars and rep ties waited deferentially. One of them held the door for the candidate.

"I'm afraid we had to let the chauffeur go," said Dr. Sutcliffe brightly. "The fellow should have known better."

When Pudge and the two young campaign assistants were safely outside he turned back to me. I noticed that for once his dentures were firmly in place. I also got the impression that he was enjoying the supremacy that grief had awarded him, however temporarily.

"My dear, I do sincerely thank you. I don't know what happened here, but the poor man does indeed look better.

84

If he has unburdened himself to you I know you will not disabuse your position of trust."

I felt like looking around for a cue card. Somebody had to be writing his lines. I just hoped it wasn't the same person who was writing Pudge's speeches, or the campaign was doomed.

"Just tea and sympathy," I said airily. "That's all *I* ever prescribe."

I had to hand it to the doctor. I'd tried to jab him, but he was too adept at handling needles to even acknowledge my attempt. He leaned back in the open door, a twinkle in his cool and ancient eyes.

"The Governor asked me to remind you," he told me, "that he is still waiting for your report."

I watched from the window as the limousine pulled away. I hoped my neighbors were watching and realized how important I was. Maybe now they would stop pestering me about the plague of dandelions on my lawn.

Chapter Twelve

Fred Astaire was dancing on the ceiling. That's the last thing I remember before nodding out in front of the tube. When that happens the dreams that follow never last longer than a thirty-second commercial break, and make just about as much sense. In one I was Ginger Rogers selling hemorrhoid cream as I tap-danced over a cobblestone street. The cobblestones were the tops of human skulls and they started to shine like ivory golf balls.

Richard woke me. The tube was blank and flickering when I answered the telephone.

"I was counting," he said. "It rang twenty-six times."

"What time is it, Richard?"

"Very early or very late. Take your pick."

"Well, don't try telling me anything too complicated. I think I'm still Ginger Rogers."

Richard let that one slide by. He was a present tense person; could be he'd never heard of Ginger or Fred. He obviously had something on his mind and I was awake enough to be suspicious. If Detective Stein was making up to me it was probably because he'd decided it was advantageous to have my client throttling the media for him.

"I don't know if this is bad news or good news," he told me. "But our case against Tony Steel just went down the toilet."

I said he'd better tell me all about it. He did. It took a while and I thought I could hear a couple of beers in his voice. Maybe the late hours were getting to him. Maybe he was having trouble with his wife Anne. I decided that was none of my business and kept my thoughts in line by taking copious notes.

When I finally hung up, light was just starting to bleed through the blue edge of night. I decided I'd had enough of the telephone and would pay a personal visit to Alfred O'Hare. If I was lucky he'd treat me to breakfast in that magnificent dining room overlooking the bluff and the sea beyond.

As I unlocked the door to my car I looked up the empty street and realized this was the second day in a row that had seen me up before cock crow. Maybe I should take up raising chickens. It would give me something to do and it would take the neighbors' thoughts off my unmowed lawn.

Since I was in a mood for crime, I pulled over at the end of the block and swiped a half-dozen tea roses from Mrs. Hendriks's prize rose bush. I imagined tracer bullets whizzing by, and a host of sirens.

The tea roses were for my mother. The parish cemetery is on the way to Sankaty Head and it had been a while since I stopped by.

I'm not much for saying prayers. Besides, there was dew on the grass and I had on my best wool skirt. It would never do to appear at the Head with grass stains on my knees, so I propped the tea roses on the headstone. There were flowers in bloom all over her little plot. It was that way from April until October because my father had a perfect genius for perpetual care.

As I approached the Head I began to get glimpses of the golf course. The light was still new over the green fairways and tendrils of ground fog reached up from the hollows. It has been three years since I picked up a club in earnest, having buried the impulse under a lot of bad memories. Still, the course where I'd learned the game has that old allure, probably because when I learned to play there it was still a game—not a business. Also, I'm loyal enough to wonder how they manage to keep the place at a championship level without my father there to direct the ground crews. I guess we can all be replaced; not always a comforting thought.

You have to slow down on the narrow bend of road that runs parallel to the seventh green. The seventh is a par three of two hundred and ten yards. I remember it very well because in the summer of my seventeenth year I holed it in one, using a new three-wood with an added swing weight. The shot helped me take the New England Juniors and convinced me that someday I would turn professional. It was a lucky hole for me, despite my abortive career.

It had not been so lucky for Byron O'Hare, who had designed the course himself. There is a shallow, spring-fed pond to the left of the big, shoulder-high bunker and he had drowned in it in the spring of 1952. When I was a kid the caddies used to say that Byron's ghost had snatched the ball whenever one of us hooked a shot into the pond.

On impulse I slowed to a stop and took a good look. There was nothing spooky about the hole, not even when the wet grass was giving up wisps of the morning fog. Maybe it was visiting my mother's grave that had put me in a peculiar frame of mind; whatever the reason, I couldn't help thinking that Byron had been lucky to die when he did. He had missed the plague of misfortune that had settled on his clan in the years after his body was found floating in the eelgrass. He had missed his sister Louise's suicide, and his niece-in-law Elisha's breakdown and confinement, and his grandnephew Alfie's drunken accident. And now he had missed the brutal murder of the grandniece who was born the year he drowned.

I was still thinking about Byron when I rang the chime at the west entrance to the main house. One of the big oak doors swung inward a few moments later. I didn't know the maid who admitted me, but apparently she recognized me because she did not appear to be surprised at my calling at six in the morning.

"Good morning, Constance."

I started involuntarily and wondered if Dr. Sutcliffe ever slept, or if he stayed up nights practicing how to appear out of the woodwork. He certainly knew how to make me feel ill at ease. Apparently he enjoyed doing so, because as we drifted toward the kitchens I caught him examining his pale image in the plate glass mirrors that line the hall.

"Himself is dressing," he explained. "I assume you're here to give him your report?"

"A verbal report, Doctor."

That put his eyebrows up. He was a man who liked things put down on paper, neatly typed, and footnoted. I think he considered me a kind of glorified secretary and was a little offended that I refused to behave like one.

My hopes of breakfasting in the firmal dining room were quickly deflated. The Governor took his fresh-squeezed orange juice and goat milk in a service nook adjacent to the kitchens.

"*Goat* milk? You've got to be kidding."

Sutcliffe compressed his waxy lips. "Not at all, my dear. The Governor does not believe in a large morning meal. For the last thirty years or so he has kept a goat. One of the cooks milks it—which can be a rather dangerous extraction, so they tell me—and that is the Governor's sustenance until noon."

I don't even like cow milk and my very limited experience with goats left the impression of ill-tempered, aromatic animals of irritating and constant voice. I hoped they would allow me a scrambled egg and a piece of toast, hold the wheat germ, and mentioned as much to Sutcliffe as he led me through the kitchens and into the "nook," which was only slightly smaller than my apartment.

"You can have anything you like. Except the goat milk. The goat gives only enough for the Governor."

"What a shame. And just when I had my heart set on a goat milk omelette."

Someone from the kitchen brought in a pot of tea and a plate of scones. I slathered whipped butter over the pastry and was happily munching away when Alfred O'Hare joined me. It was a novelty to breakfast with a man wearing a suit and firmly knotted tie. I would have thought the knot would make it hard to get the goat milk down, but the Governor had thirty years of practice and he quaffed the hot, repulsive stuff with nary a shudder.

"Something has happened," he said, patting his lips with a linen napkin. "Tell me about it."

Reconstructing a crime from a pathologist's report is a tricky business. With all the muttering Richard and Tim Rosen had done about blood types I thought they had stumbled on some kind of exotic problem, or maybe a way of accurately pegging the separate times of the two deaths. But what it came down to was a Banlon shirt heavily encrusted with two types of blood. The shirt was the one Jon Maxfield had been wearing when he was killed. Some of the blood was his own, which had seeped from the deep back wound that severed his aorta. The rest of the blood was spattered all over his chest, and the coroner had determined that it was Mandy's blood. The spattering was consistent with that produced by a live blood vessel.

The Governor appeared to be genuinely puzzled. "I'm missing something here," he told me. "Can you tell me what this means, in layman's language?"

"It means that Jon Maxfield stabbed Mandy. Or that is how Tony Steel's lawyers will present the evidence if Steel is brought to trial for Mandy's homicide."

It was interesting to watch the storm clouds forming in the old gentleman's eyes. His thick white brows began to tremble and I almost expected lightning to start flashing.

"This is preposterous." The mug of goat milk rattled as he put it down. "I had thought that Jew detective was a bright lad, but this sounds . . . do you mean to tell me that Sicilian pimp they arrested will get off scot-free?"

"Not at all. He's to be arraigned and charged with stabbing Jon Maxfield."

Now the brows were waggling and the cool blue eyes, much younger than the craggy face, were looking askance.

"The scenario goes like this," I said, repeating words Richard had used earlier that morning. "The prosecution will endeavor to prove that Mandy had some kind of drug-related dealings with Maxfield and possibly with Tony Steel. That Maxfield stabbed Mandy and left her on the bed. Possibly this was witnessed by Tony Steel, but that is conjecture. It is also conjecture, logically assumed, that Tony Steel followed Maxfield outside to the alley and then stabbed him, possibly in revenge for killing Mandy."

I could see him taking it in, mulling it over, and then hardening himself to the information. I didn't like it any better than he did. And I knew that Stein was none too enthusiastic, either. But the prosecutor was convinced that the coroner's report absolutely ruined the case against Steel having stabbed Mandy. What I didn't want to go into right then was how weak the merits were of the case against Steel having killed Maxfield. Richard had assured me that he would be held for at least another three days before a bail hearing would set bond, and that probably it would be set high enough to keep him inside while Stein and Rosen tried to put another case together.

"This stinks," said Alfred O'Hare. "I've seen better things on television. Who's the coroner, that addle-brained Nesmith?"

"He has a good reputation," I said without much conviction. "He's very good in testimony."

"I remember him," said the Governor darkly. "At the inquest when Byron drowned. A ghoul."

I hadn't realized that Nesmith had been with the coroner's office for so many years. He must have been right out of medical school when Byron died. The world and time seemed to be shrinking together. I drank another cup of tea and ate another scone to settle my stomach.

"I'm afraid I woke up in a very uncharitable mood," said the Governor. "Because it again occurs to me that if little Mandy had wanted to spoil her father's chances she's done an excellent job of it."

It wasn't just the statement, it was the timbre of the voice behind it that made my skin crawl. Maybe because I've never had a passion for politics and therefore lack the necessary perspective to understand how totally consuming is the quest for office and power. In her own way, to the best of her limited ability, Mandy O'Hare had been a friend to me, and in the week I'd been on the case I had yet to hear anyone lament her passing. Oh, Pudge had cried tears, but I suspected they had been fueled by Scotch and physical exhaustion. More than that, he mourned the girl he remembered as a child, not the woman who had been an adult, in the most fundamental sense, since she was fourteen. It was not only depressing, it made me a little angry.

"You're right, of course," said her grandfather genially, when I mentioned it to him. "We *are* beasts. It's in the blood, I fear, and no one had it more plainly than the girl you call your friend. I believe you got a taste of her manipulative talents, once upon a time?"

92

The son of a bitch. So the old lizard had known all along and had waited to insert that little comment with the precision of an acupuncturist.

"Grampa," said a sleepy voice. "You're being mean again."

Kitty had come into the breakfast nook. She was carrying a pitcher of orange juice and was wearing a cotton tee-shirt and a pair of panties that had seen better days. The contrast to her stiff-backed grandfather in his flawless suit and firmly knotted tie was impressive.

"You're right, kitten," he said amiably. "I'm a mean old grampa. But our good friend Constance has made a profession of dealing with meanies like me, so I'm reasonably sure I haven't really hurt her feelings."

I assumed it was as close as the Governor ever got to an apology. It was backhanded and self-serving, but then I couldn't expect the old tiger to change his stripes for me, when he hadn't been able to for Mandy.

"Look, it's going to be a long day." I stood up, dusting the scone crumbs off my skirt. "I'll be in touch."

I had a few questions I wanted to ask Kitty. I thought she might be responsive because she knew by now that I hadn't snitched about her assignation with Bo Bernardi. But there was no point in asking when her grandfather was there, so I flashed her what I hoped was a trusting smile and made my excuses.

"Kitty would see you to the door," said the Governor, "but she's forgotten to wear her bathrobe again, hasn't she?"

"Oh Alfred, please shut up."

My father was in his garden. He was sitting on a sturdy wooden bench, hoeing at a neat row of asparagus sprouts. The wheelchair was beside the bench. He has the raw strength to move himself about with his arms and hands, although he has been warned many times about the risk of overexertion.

"Hi, Pop. It's me, the prodigal daughter."

I'd like to think it wasn't guilt that made me stop by on the way back from the Head. Having made my homage to the dead, I naturally tried to seek a balance by visiting the living. Maybe I should skip the ponderous excuses and admit that being a daughter is almost as tough as being a parent. Not that I know the parenting part from personal experience.

My father had given up on the speech therapy and there was no point in trying to push him back into it. He was taciturn by nature and the loss of his speaking voice seemed to trouble me more than it did him. When he had something that needed saying he either managed to communicate it physically or, if necessary, wrote it in a spiral-bound notebook he carried everywhere.

"Guess what, Pop? I just had breakfast with your old pal, the former governor."

By the way he nodded I knew that he was aware of the work I was doing for the O'Hares. Probably one of his cronies from the golf course. You can't keep a secret in the vicinity of Sankaty Head, where idle gossip has been developed into an art form.

My father pantomimed knotting a tie, tilting his nose back with a patrician air. That made me laugh; he's a good mimic when he wants to be.

"You've got him down pat. Did you know the old reprobate drinks goat milk for breakfast?"

He knew it. There wasn't a lot he didn't know about the O'Hare family, having worked for them for the best part of his life. In better years he had flown with Pudge to new developments under construction all over the country, where his expertise in greenskeeping and cultivation was required. And when I was a kid he was close enough to the family to be asked to make up a foursome with Alfred and

Pudge and Dr. Sutcliffe. I believe the object of the match play was a "gentlemen's wager" and my father, a scratch golfer, was the ringer.

I might mention here that neither of the Alfreds was a good player, despite their having been responsible for the layout and construction of more than twenty of the best modern courses in America. Pudge had a pretty looking swing, all style and thunder, and an incurable slice. His father could hit the ball straight, but couldn't putt for beans.

I was in my early teens when the foursome dissolved; rumor had it the argument was on account of one of the foursome cheating. My father refused to comment one way or the other and naturally I sided with my family. I took it seriously enough to cease going to the Head. Although Mandy paid little heed to what she considered the mere sputterings of adult discontent, we gradually drifted apart.

It wasn't until I was grown up and found myself struggling on the Women's Professional Golf Tour circuit that I wondered if my father had been the one accused of cheating. As the only pauper of the four he had the most to lose. It was an unworthy thought that came to me as I struggled to resist my own temptation to cheat by, say, scuffing a rough-hacked ball a crucial yard closer to the fairway. The wince of shame at the mere thought of what would happen if I were caught prevented me from trying surreptitiously to cut a few strokes off my score.

"Okay." I saw the speculative glint in my father's eye. "You've got something planned. You better spill it."

He worked himself back into the chair and would not allow me to push as he rolled the contraption toward the garage, where he kept his workshop. He had had an automatic opener installed and the rickety panels creaked upward when he pressed the signal button. The shop had never been off limits, though it had been a while since I'd had a reason to prowl around in there, and I was not surprised to see that nothing had changed. He still had the wood lathe and the band saw and a king-sized rack of carving tools.

The other thing he still had was a lot of nerve. I saw the set of woods immediately, the new varnish gleaming under the shop lights. He picked the driver up, polished the head with the corner of his flannel shirt, and put the grip so near to my hands I could not refuse.

It was a beautiful job, of course. No one had ever bought a custom set of woods from Johnny Kale because he would not sell them. A lucky few had, over the years, got them as presents. This would be my second set, the first being the half-sized sticks I played with until I outgrew them at twelve or thirteen. God knew how many months he'd been working on the set.

"Pop, they're gorgeous. I appreciate the thought but you know I don't—"

I had to stop because he was writing something in his notebook. Grinning, he tore out the sheet and handed it to me.

These are just for fun, princess.
Happy Birthday!

When I'd finished sniffling I gave the crafty old son-of-a-gun a hug. He had a point. It was time I got over the hurt of not being good enough and rediscovered the physical joy the game had given me as a girl. We went back out into the garden so he could watch me try them out.

"Don't expect much, Pop. It's been four years since I took a full cut."

I took a few experimental swings with the three-wood. It was perfectly weighted for me, and precisely shafted. I put some zip into it, shaving the grass, and we both heard the clean *swish* sound of a quality head. My father nodded, satisfied with himself and me, and made the thumbs-up sign.

96

"It's not my birthday, you know."

He shrugged. With him a birthday was whenever he remembered one.

After that I couldn't just light out on him, so I plopped myself down and watched him tend the garden. We chatted for an hour or so, me yakking and him listening, which had been how it was long before the stroke silenced his speaking voice.

I had the new set of woods wrapped in chamois and was getting ready to leave when I remembered that I had a question for him.

"Pop, I slowed down to take a look at the old seventh hole early this morning. How exactly was it that Byron O'Hare drowned in that shallow pond?"

It might have been my imagination, but I thought his sun-drenched, leathery face paled for a moment. I could sense the wheels spinning and the clock turning back. On a sheet in his notebook he scrawled:

Go ask Win Browning.

Browning was the club pro. In the old days he had been an assistant greenskeeper under my father. I suspected that he could have answered the question himself, but wanted to put me and my new clubs in close proximity to the first tee.

I wasn't about to tell him that his scheme had no chance of working. If I tried out his "birthday" presents anywhere it would be in the privacy of my own backyard, in the dead of night.

Chapter Thirteen

Had I been more observant I would probably have noticed the Toyota earlier in the day. As it was, the green
wagon did not register until I looked into the rearview
while pulling out of the Sankaty Head club house parking
lot. Win Browning was giving a lesson and I had decided
not to wait. My verbal contract with Alfred O'Hare was to
cover an investigation into the particulars of his granddaughter's death. What happened to Uncle Byron thirty
years before was curiosity I'd have to satisfy on my own
time.

The road from the Head to Rivermuth skirts the
beaches, winding along the coast. At an intersection I
turned left, off the main road, tromped on the pedal for a
quarter of a mile, and then pulled over on the wrong side
of a blind curve. A minute or so later the green Toyota
came chugging by. I pulled out behind the car, recognized
the driver, and had to laugh. I pulled up tight on his
bumper, leaned on the horn, and waved him over to the
side of the road.

"Hi there, Truman, what a coincidence."

He stayed in his car while I put a hip on the fender. His small triangular face was a blushing shade of pink and he was having trouble meeting my eyes.

"It's not what you think, Connie," he said in a very low voice.

"That depends," I said, "on what you think I think. Would you like to know what I think you think I think?"

No answer. I folded my elbows on the side of the door, facing him through the rolled-down window.

"I think you're following me, True Blue."

It was a nickname Richard Stein had given him, and from the way Hawkins reacted I knew it struck a nerve.

"What if I was?" he said.

"Well, hypothetically speaking, I'd say there was not much I could do about it. But this is not a hypothetical world, Tru. If I wanted I could file a harassment complaint. Or complain to your editor."

That put some steel in his spine. I could see him recovering his composure. "Your client already did that," he said. "Called my editor."

"And what was the reaction at the *Record,* mighty bastion of freedom that it is?"

"Aw, come on, I know the paper stinks. I'm doing the best job I can. On my own, sort of."

Truman was still a little sweet on me and it wasn't difficult to wheedle it out of him. His paper, owned by a chain of suburban dailies, had not been interested in tangling with the O'Hares over a mere news item. Had it been an advertising account, they'd have gone to the canvas; as it was Truman was advised to find another story to file.

He was a small man of delicate sentiment, who disliked being dictated to, especially over a story that had, as he put it, some meat to it. He did as his editor requested, so far as the *Record* was concerned. At the same time he was following up on the story with hopes of selling a free-lance piece to the Sunday magazine section of the *Portland Herald.*

"And what did they say at the *Herald*?" I asked him.

"No commitment," he admitted. "But they'll look at what I have. Once I get the story in shape. Aw, come on, Connie, I could use a break."

No doubt about that. However much I might have liked to help him out, Alfred O'Hare was paying me a handsome per diem to do just the opposite. I said as much.

"You could be an unnamed source, Connie."

"Truman, you've been reading *All the President's Men* again. Believe me, I'm no Deep Throat. The Governor would be on to me by the time he finished reading your lead paragraph."

The reporter was insistent. I sensed a stubbornness in him I'd not previously noticed. When he mentioned "mutual cooperation" I was curious enough to want him to spell it out.

"Hey, don't get the idea I'm trying to play detective. It's just there are a couple of interesting things."

"Such as?"

"Trade me?"

"You go first."

Truman had done a pretty fair job on background. He had interviewed Kitty, gotten a rather surly statement from Bo Bernardi, a deposition from the manager of the Birmingham, and a bushel basket of gossip from jealous neighbors in and around Sankaty Head.

"I know Pudge has been drunk for six days," he said rather smugly.

"Not true," I lied. "The candidate has not taken a drink in many years."

"Sure. Since the day they took Elisha away in the little white wagon, right? Be that as it may, the poor sap has been swimming in a vat of Scotch."

I had to give him credit. He had the type of booze

right. Once I got him started he kept bubbling. I felt the small teeth of nibbling guilt for getting him to spill when I had no intention of reciprocating. I don't think he really minded; he was excited about the story and eager to share it with someone, anyone, even with me.

"You know what's really fishy?" he asked me. I was about to say chowder, then thought better of it. "That marriage to Bernardi. Did you know those two never even lived together? And that the little sister was hot for Bo right from the start?"

I protested my ignorance and tried, rather half-heartedly, to convince Hawkins that rumors to that effect were not only hideous, but untrue.

"Come on, don't kid me. I bet you know all about it, being one of that crowd from way back."

It wasn't all that flattering to be mistaken for one of the Sankaty Head crowd. I was just becoming convinced that Truman had nothing new to tell me when he mentioned Mandy's mother.

"Now *that's* an odd thing, of itself," he said in his sober way. "I don't suppose you'd give me the tiniest reason for why Mandy went to visit her mom, eh?"

I held my expression as it was. Fortunately I'd been pretending ignorance, so when the real thing surfaced Truman didn't notice.

"On the very day she was to get murdered. Now isn't that pretty melodramatic stuff? I tell you, Connie, that whole family belongs in a museum. Or maybe in there in the loony bin with the mother, you know?"

When in doubt, wisecrack. I told Truman I had an appointment in Samara and that he could follow me anywhere as long as he gave me Arpège. And wouldn't you know that the little encyclopedia would have a response for that.

"You know what ambergris is?" he said deadpan.

"That stuff they put in perfume? It's just whale vomit, Connie. That's why I never give a girl perfume. I got better taste than *that*."

I gave up. The green wagon followed me along the beach road. I slowed down a few times, pretending to look for stranded leviathans, but Truman didn't get it.

Chapter Fourteen

Shorty had a special on barbecued ribs. Could be it was gnawing hunger that made them taste so good, but licking my fingertips as I waited for seconds, I thought even Calvin Trillin would have given the sauce his stamp of approval.

"Boy, oh boy," said Shorty as he loomed down with the second plate. "Doan I love a broad witha appetite."

The women's movement has passed Shorty by without disturbing one hair of his salt-and-pepper, Marine-camp crewcut. The last time he had his consciousness raised was in an elevator; I liked him anyway.

"So what's the secret, Connie?" he said, dropping his voice seriously. "You in one of those physical fitness programs? Is that how you keep skinny like a rail and still eat like a healthy racehorse?"

I proposed marriage. Shorty was fattening up his third wife and declined. By way of making up he placed one of his small Greek salads to one side of the rib plate and covered the fresh lettuce and olives with a healthy dose of his special salad dressing. Secret police with electric prodders couldn't have gotten the recipe out of him.

"Some things is destined to be between a man and his Maker," he was fond of saying when asked to give over a list of ingredients. "Believe me, this dressing I invented could make me a millionaire if only I weren't too tall to appear on television."

I was wiping the last drop up with a triangle of Syrian bread when the band started playing.

"Good Lord," I said when a bugle trilled loud enough to rattle my fillings.

"Nah," said Shorty. "It ain't the Salvation Army."

I swiveled on my stool and saw a drum and bugle corps milling around the square, waiting for two uniformed cops to stop traffic. A couple of skinny kids from the bugle corps unfurled a banner, which flapped in the slight breeze.

"You're right, Shorty," I said. "Not God but politics."

Specifically it was the campaign for Pudge O'Hare. Apparently working from the premise that everyone loves a parade, the O'Hare campaign people had put together something I was pretty sure they'd call a "miniparade"—six bugles, three drums, and three majorettes who might have been triplets. They formed in the square around a convertible limousine. In the back seat of the limo, waving a straw hat, was the candidate.

The man who had wept boozy tears in my humble little kitchen was now out in the streets, shaking hands from the slowly moving vehicle and flashing his pearly whites like a heavyweight champ. He made me want to run up and get his autograph, or maybe check his breath. I had to admire the physical stamina that had enabled him to recover so quickly. Had I been on a monster five-day drunk like Pudge it would have taken me at least a month to recover. Not the second of the Alfreds. He was radiating health and goodwill. Seeing him campaign in the flesh rather than on the slick, plastic video spots, I thought maybe he really did have the stuff to win the primary. He looked solid, respectable, and slightly larger than life.

I pushed myself away from the empty blue-plate special and went out into the square. The Governor was nowhere to be seen; maybe they thought he'd be a liability, a reminder of many failed campaigns. The little parade circled the fountain, attracting the attention of the noontime strollers, many of whom allowed their hands to be shaken by the would-be Congressman. The bugles were tootling something that had once belonged to John Philip Sousa. It sounded like Sousa had disposed of the tune and the buglers had dug it up and were trying to figure out how it worked. The drummers ignored the fun and just kept bashing. The citizens in the square seemed to like what was going on; many were smiling, a few local comedians were pretending to cover their ears. All in all there was a distinct small town feel to the parade, which was much more attractive than the television spots.

The limo tooled around the square until the buglers had exhausted their repertoire, or were just plain exhausted, and came to stop at a storefront festooned with banners. That was the Rivermuth campaign headquarters and red, white, and blue bunting suggested that everyone "Meet the Candidate" and partake of free coffee and homemade doughnuts.

Somehow I couldn't see Kitty slaving away in the kitchen over the pastry, but the sentiment was nice.

By a gradual process of attrition the trading center of Rivermuth has moved away from the river, leaving behind abandoned warehouses and tumbling brick buildings that have only recently been renovated into expensive apartments and chic little shops. Having very little interest in the two-hundred-dollar pleated preppy skirts displayed in the shop windows, or the three hundred varieties of wax candles available right next door, I naturally gravitated to the river itself.

A trawler, low in the water, was thumping up river against the tide. The gulls wheeling overhead looked like white leaves stirred up by a whirlwind. At an ancient pier rock salt was being unloaded from a rust-encrusted freighter; great scoops of the stuff were being dumped from steam shovels onto the peak of a small white mountain. Beyond the salt pile is an inland harbor area. You can see the black spars thrusting up from the mud where there had once been a drydock, back in the days of sailing vessels. An old, prewar bridge spans the deepest part of the river. People had been known to jump from that bridge; that afternoon the rails were empty.

For no good reason the empty bridge reminded me that Louise O'Hare had drowned herself in the family swimming pool. She had been determined enough to tie a rope of lead sashweights around her waist before walking off the deep end. Maybe she'd been inspired by the example of her drowned brother, Byron.

As I made my leisurely way back into the center of town I was thinking that True Blue Hawkins had a point when he said the whole family ought to be locked away in a museum, or in the sanitarium with Elisha. It was not a generous thought and might well have been prompted by a subconscious fear that by working so near to the source of misery, I might catch a dose of it myself.

The risks of the job. As I came in range of the Rivermuth Police Station an unmarked cruiser pulled up beside me and a certain handsome and married detective rolled down the driver's side window.

"I stopped by your place," he said reproachfully. "Nobody home."

"Really? And just when I thought there was another one of me back there mopping the floors and airing out the featherduster."

Richard was in no mood for lame jokes. His department had just gotten a rocket from the law firm representing the O'Hares. Threats of a civil suit had been unfurled only an hour or so before Pudge's banners hit the breeze.

"That's it," he told me. "No more favors. No more helpful hints."

I tried to reason with him. Alfred O'Hare made a habit of unleashing his law firm on innocent bystanders. Usually nothing came of it and O'Hare's civil suits against public servants were almost always withdrawn. I promised to do what I could to appease the old boy's temper. Meanwhile it would only further infuriate the Governor if Stein and his men refused to cooperate.

"So you've got it all figured out, have you?" he snapped before I was quite done. "Well let me spell it out for you. My department was cooperating with the O'Hares—through you—because it did not behoove us to be in an antagonistic posture to a family with their influence. Sound funny? That's because I am quoting the memo the chief sent me. Now let me quote his latest memo. 'Any person representing former Governor Alfred O'Hare or his attorneys is to be shown the door.' Period."

"But Richard, I never even got *inside* the door."

"You know what, Connie? Nobody likes a wise guy. And nobody at all likes a wise-guy woman, okay? So lay off it."

It was a nice try, but at times like that my mouth speaks for itself. "Does this mean you won't be calling at four in the morning, Richard?"

I thought he was going to give me one right back, which would have been better in the long run. Instead he swallowed whatever he was about to say, shook his head ruefully, and stalked into the station house.

I had two problems. The first was that I no longer had a feed in the department. If I wanted access to the files I would have to break in. The second was that I wasn't sure I was ready to see the last of Richard Stein, married or not. Rationally I knew that the break was a good thing, in regard to the second problem, but it left me without a solution to the first. I felt like a tired swimmer fighting a tidal current, not yet ready to go down.

It looked like a good afternoon to get out of town. I was feeling spunky and nervous and the barbecued ribs were starting to repeat. Rolling the windows down I kept the Duster's speed at a mere six miles per hour over the limit, and tried to let the white lines hypnotize me. That worked so well that I missed the Portland exit and had to get off at Falmouth and track back. The last time I'd been to Portland was to pay a visit to the Ranchero Lounge and Dance. This time I was in no mood for four-hundred-pound wrestlers or smarmy hoodlums like Arnold Maury.

If there is a city in New England that does not have a neighborhood of three-story wooden tenements, complete with sagging porches stacked in triplicate the better to air your own laundry while spying on the neighbors' dirty linen, I have yet to visit it.

I happen to favor the style, which probably proves my lack of taste and architectural sophistication. I like it because people live there, sometimes three generations in the same building, certainly on the same block. Invariably the neighborhood has a corner store that sells beer and baby food in equal quantities, and the people who live there think a boutique is some dumb flower the kids pin on each other on prom night. The kids in the street still know how to play ring-a-levio without ever being told the rules by adults and the girls still toughen up their knees playing hopscotch, which comes in handy nowadays because some of those same girls are playing in the Little League and on the school football teams.

Mrs. Ruth Palowski, a widow, had the middle floor of a building that was painted in three different bands of colors, which made me suspect that the three floors were separately owned. Mrs. Palowski, smelling heavily of lavender and girdle, confirmed the suspicion.

"Mr. Floris over and Miss Keeley—she never married—is under. So are you from the city directory? Or is it the census again?"

The door was already wide open and Mrs. Palowski had me firmly by the elbow, dragging me inside. I got the impression she was looking for verbal intercourse with someone—anyone. She had a little blue bun of hair, half-moon spectacles she might have borrowed from my late mother, and just the trace of a Polish accent all mixed up with the mysterious *r*'s and *h*'s of the northeast coast.

"It's about your son Randy, Mrs. Palowski," I said gently, sitting precariously on the edge of a sofa that wanted to engulf me. "Is he in?"

"Randy?" her eyes widened into a smile. "Oh goodness, I tink you got the wrong Palowski. My son is Joseph. His Confirmation saint was Timothy."

"Randy is a stage name?" That was a guess. I'd gotten the address from the Steel file and a glance around the sitting room convinced me Mrs. Palowski had lived here for many years.

She seemed happy at the guess. "Oh, my Joe is on the stage, many times on the stage. Now I tink he travels with this play, very popular. He tells me he sings nice songs, and also he dances to modern music."

I could vouch for the modern music. I tuned in my most ingenuous expression, not that it was really required, and asked if I might see a snapshot of Joseph, saint name Timothy. The widow Palowski couldn't have been more delighted. She glided over to a bookcase that seemed to hold the combined publishing efforts of *Reader's Digest* and *National Geographic,* removed four large vinyl-covered photo albums, and arranged them on the coffee table.

"My goodness. Now I know that every mama tinks her

son is handsome—that happens the moment you give birth. But my Joseph, he was always such a pretty boy."

I wasn't going to be the one to tell her he was still a pretty boy. There had been no mistake, I was looking at the picture-story life of Randy "the Rogue" Palowski. About two hundred fading Kodaks of Randy in diapers, as a toddler, caught in mid-blubber as he was about to enter first grade. I told Mrs. Palowski I agreed that he was terribly cute at ten, his face covered with mustard at a family picnic, handsome indeed in his gown of Confirmation white two years later.

"The Bishop slapped his cheek," she explained.

"What?" All sorts of weird scenarios came to mind. Passion in the vestry, drama in the confessional booth.

"It's part of the Holy Ceremony," she intoned. "The Bishop slaps the boys who are getting confirmed. It means they are soldiers for Christ. My Joe looked like an angel. Of course he always had a little of the devil in him. All boys do."

When I looked into her eyes I saw the question there. Mrs. Palowski was a sweet woman and a doting mother, but she was not a fool. She wanted to know if a little of the devil in Randy had got into me.

"Mrs. Palowski, I don't know your son personally," I explained. "I'm a free-lance journalist and I specialize in doing theater reviews. You know, profile sort of things?"

I thought my nose was growing at about an inch per word, but it was exactly what Mrs. Palowksi wanted to hear. I could almost feel her relief from the anxiety she had been covering up with her chatter. She launched into a biography of Joseph Timothy and thoughtfully provided me with pencil and paper, the better to take notes.

After thirty minutes of nodding and scribbling, I determined that Randy had been living at home off and on. Until about a week ago it had been on, at which time he packed up and went to stay at a beach cottage for the duration of one of his theatrical experiences.

"He doesn't drive, you know. Automobiles make Joe very nervous. He got that from me."

"You say a beach cottage. Did he tell you what beach? I really *would* like to interview him personally. At home, you know, relaxing."

By then I'd half convinced myself that I really was taking notes for a profile. Mrs. Palowski assured me that Joe would give her a call just as soon as he had a telephone put in, but you know how difficult the phone company can be. She was vague about the beach, so I named a few.

"Ogunquit? Old Orchard? York?"

"No, something to do with sand. You know, like Sandy. Joe says it's very hoity-toity, wealthy people."

"Sankaty Head?"

"That's it!" said Mrs. Palowski happily. "Joe is renting a pretty little cottage at Sankaty Head. Now if you'll wait here a minute I'll see if I can find the name of the landlord. I made Joe write it down for me."

Sankaty Head. I'd not been surprised to discover that Randy the Rogue had gone on the lam. An aversion to cops and murder/drug investigations is not uncommon. The one thing I hadn't expected to find was that he'd crept back into the lion's den.

Mrs. Palowski returned from her bedroom carrying a fat address book. She put it on the table and sorted through bits of ink-strewn paper.

"Here it is. The man who owns the cottage Joe is renting is named Gerald Sutcliffe. I tink you look surprise, dear. You know him?"

Oh, I knew him. Gerald was the eldest of Dr. Sutcliffe's two children, first cousin to Mandy O'Hare, and the last time I'd seen him he'd been wearing a dress.

Chapter Fifteen

The Duster blew a gasket a mile or two east of the Rivermuth exit. My ankles were feeling hot and sweaty, and when I reached down to open the air vent I saw clouds of steam rolling up around my knees. If I hadn't been so distracted by the connection between cousin Gerald and Randy the Rogue I might have noticed the thermostat dial was all the way in the red.

By the time I'd pulled over the steam was boiling out from under the hood and the engine block was clanking and making metallic noises that I associated with automotive death. My attitude towards automobiles is one of bemused resignation, so long as they are in running order. When one breaks down I want to blow it up.

"Too late for that," said the highway patrolman who stopped and put out flares while I waited for the tow truck. "Looks to me like she seized up pretty good."

The tow truck attendant, a boy of eighteen or so, wearing a Red Sox hat and overalls that smelled of gasoline, was even more to the point. He wrinkled a few pimples, picked idly at the side of his nose, and said in a laconic, throaty baritone, "Lady, this car is history."

All they charged me for towing the wreck two miles was eighty dollars.

"But that's highway robbery!" I protested to the boy's boss who, from the look of him, was also the boy's father. He just shrugged and took my money. Cash, no checks, thanks. The boy, who had a humorous sparkle in his gray eyes, started chuckling.

"Hey lady," he said. "Hey that's a good one. I gotta remember that. You get it, Pop? Highway robbery?"

I left because it looked like the explanation might take a while. I found a payphone and spent four dollars and an hour's frustration arranging for a rental car. I decided to put it on Alfred O'Hare's bill, since he was a member in good standing of the capitalist establishment that had manufactured the blown gasket, and therefore shared in the collective fault. My reasoning was probably as faulty as the gasket, but it helped to keep me from strangling myself with the telephone cord.

By the time I got back to Rivermuth I was in no mood to look up Gerald Sutcliffe or Randy Joe Palowski, and I was certainly in no mood to deal with Truman Hawkins, who had parked his green and gasket-sound Toyota across the street from my place.

"I'll be darned," he said, his hands deep in his pockets and his eyes bugging out more than usual. "You went and rented a car to shake me!"

I'd have rented a Waring to blend him had one of sufficient size been available.

"Some other time, Truman," I growled, fishing for the door keys. My stomach started falling when I realized I'd left the key on the same ring that was still in the ignition of the junked Duster.

"Aw, Connie. I didn't mean to make you cry."

"These are tears of rage, Truman."

As a reporter he was no great shakes. As a house-breaker he had possibilities. The small window pane he broke needed cleaning anyhow. For that act of gallantry I felt obliged to offer him a drink.

"Nah. Just maybe some ice water for me," he said with an edge to his voice. "I'm off the stuff. I have this allergic reaction to alcohol."

It seemed, by the nervous way he paced the living room, that he had an allergic reaction to being alone with me. I kind of liked Truman and wanted to put him at ease. I took a slow, shuddering sip of my bourbon on the rocks and another swig from the glass of iced soda water.

"So tell me," I said. "How did you happen to be in the neighborhood?"

That was only slightly better than inquiring about the weather. From the tight set of Truman's mouth I didn't think he even heard what I said. His bulbous forehead made it look as though his mind were swelling with agitated thoughts.

"It's the ten grand, Connie. That's what I can't figure. That's what doesn't make sense. I mean if he *knew* the guy had the money why not take it? And if he *didn't* know then why did he kill him?"

A bourbon heat wave was passing through my body. Although I'm not a heavy drinker, there are times when one sturdy glass can be an elixir. I was concentrating on the feeling and what Truman said didn't immediately register.

"Back up, please," I said, putting my tired feet up on the ottoman. "What ten thousand? Kill who for what ten thousand?"

A couple of emotions passed rapidly through the reporter's shining eyes. Surprise, incredulity, maybe a touch of triumph he quickly squelched because he thought I was putting him on.

114

"You know. The ten grand they found in Maxfield's wallet."

I could see that foggy alley and the bright lights. Richard rolling over the body, the sound of fabric tearing, and a wallet with green bills. I hadn't given a thought to the money or how much it amounted to—and Richard Stein, that so-and-so, had failed to mention that the bills were of high denomination. Ten grand? A dope payment? A dealer's bank?

Mandy's money?

"Okay, Tru. You're way ahead of me here. This is the first I heard about the ten thousand. I guess I should make a trade." About the only thing I had was Randy the Rogue camping out in a cottage owned by Mandy's first cousin. I didn't dare give him that, because the Governor would have my head on a plate if he found out I was the source. "How about this: Kitty O'Hare and Bo Bernardi are now an item."

Truman waved that away. "Come on, Connie. That's *old*. I mean thanks, but I really didn't come over here looking to trade. I know what your job is and I respect it. Like you respect me, right?"

"Right." And quite suddenly I did, a little ashamed for having assumed that his efforts were those of a bumbling amateur. Looking him over carefully, I could see that his face was drawn and pale, there were dark circles under his big eyes; the effect was of someone deprived of sleep. Yes, he was onto something hot and it was keeping him awake.

"There is something *rotten* about it, Connie. You've got stripper A and stripper B. Both of these guys are working for Arnold Maury, who has been indicted like ten times for various racketeering schemes. Indicted but never convicted. And get this—his brother is Big Mike Maury, who is a heavy on the South Portland waterfront. You want to float a loan with just your legs as collateral, you go to Big Mike."

I just kept nodding, trying to give the impression that I knew all about Big Mike the loan shark. Truman had been putting a lot of miles on that little green wagon of his. I wondered if his editor knew how much company time was going into Hawkins's free-lance efforts.

"Okay, enter a little rich girl named Mandy O'Hare. Rumor has it Mandy likes the occasional toot. Also she has been known to take strangers to bed . . ." His cheeks started getting pink and he kept his eyes directed at the floor as he paced, ticking off the points. "So what if she was buying a quantity of cocaine supplied by Arnold Maury—I guess you know he's been interrogated by the Drug Enforcement Task Force? Okay, okay, what counts is that Steel and Maxfield have this connection to Mandy. Maybe she is, ah, sleeping with both of them? Some jealousy thing? Is that possible, Connie?"

The last question was barely audible because his voice had dropped, apparently due to embarrassment or anxiety. The ten-watt bulb over my head clicked on and I knew what Truman Hawkins was doing in my living room.

"Let me get this straight," I said gently, taking another sip of the bourbon rocks. "You're asking me if it was possible that Mandy was sleeping with both Tony Steel and Jonny Maxfield?"

Truman sighed and finally collapsed onto the divan. He still couldn't meet my eyes. "Well, sort of. Aw, Connie, I know she was a friend of yours and I don't like mentioning an ugly thing like this, especially when it's still just a theory."

"Truman, please listen to me. You're a very sweet, gentle man and I appreciate your sensitivity, okay? Believe me, this discussion is not embarrassing or offending me. And to answer your questions, yes it *is* theoretically possible that Mandy was having sex with both of those guys.

116

Furthermore it is possible that she was doing it with both of them at the same time. Now isn't that what you wanted to know? If it was possible?"

The poor guy was actually hanging his head in shame. By my estimation Truman was approximately thirty years old. I'd never had reason to think about it one way or another, but now I wondered if he had any sexual experience at all. Was it possible in the late twentieth century for a man to be a virgin into his thirtieth season?

"Possible," he mumbled, as if he'd been reading my thoughts. "Physically possible."

"Truman," I said. "I don't know what happened that night at the Sea Breeze Motel. Maybe Mandy and Tony Steel and Jonny Max played a game of charades, or spin the bottle, or post office. But if she hopped in the sack with the both of them it wouldn't be the first time she had "relations" with two men at once. Not from the stories she used to tell. And if you use any of that while I'm still working for the Governor, Truman, I will be *extremely* unhappy about it. Okay?"

He nodded vigorously and had finally screwed up the courage to look me in the eye. "Never. How could I use that? That's slander, Connie. Gosh, they'd have me in court for the rest of my life."

"A good point. Please remember it when you sit down to type up the article."

"See, it's not like I need to *describe* the act. It's the ten thousand. I mean what if it *wasn't* dope money? What if it was blackmail?"

I rattled the ice in my glass. I hadn't switched on any lights or drawn up the shades and in the dim light the ice looked like diamonds in solution. Blackmail. Ten grand was a nice round figure to name as a blackmail fee. But who was blackmailing whom? And for what? Looking at Truman's anxious expression—he was making a meal of his fingernails—I assumed that the theory he was so hesitant to lay out involved Mandy being blackmailed for some kind of sexual stunt. It was possible. I knew from personal experience that Mandy was fully capable of putting on quite a show, and that when the mood was on her she didn't care how big the audience was.

"I don't know, Truman," I said after giving it some thought. "I just can't see Mandy paying off a blackmailer. She was a very open person, when it came to her sex life. She didn't care who knew about it. As a matter of fact I think she got off on making her exploits public."

Hawkins shivered. I didn't know if it was revulsion or excitement. I was beginning to think that he needed to find himself a time machine and send himself back to when reporters wore spats and black bowler hats and the closest thing to a pin-up the scandal sheets published was a rotogravure of a Gibson girl. He was altogether too delicate to be delving into the lives of the O'Hare sisters, either one of whom could have stripped Truman of his psyche in about thirty minutes.

"You think I'm a sissy, don't you?" he said abruptly. It wasn't so much an accusation as a plea for denial. "You think I'm a funny-looking little wimp, right?"

I'd have given him a kiss on the forehead except that it would have complicated matters. "I think you're a man like any other, Tru," I said truthfully, before switching gears for a little white lie. "And as a matter of fact I think you're sorta cute. The sensitive type."

It was worth it. A wave of relief radiated off the little, froglike man. Without stretching my imagination too much I could see a starched white collar around his neck. I wondered whatever had possessed him to become a reporter, traditionally one of the more cynical, not to say hardboiled, of professions.

Then again he probably wondered how I'd gotten into my line of work.

"You know, Connie," he said in a hushed voice.

118

"There are things going on here that give me the creeps. Psychos like Arnold Maury, and behavior I'll never understand, like what Mandy did, and what her sister is still doing. But dammit, the whole thing is *fascinating,* you know? It's dirty and nasty and miserable and I *like* it. Isn't that weird?"

I told him it wasn't weird at all. It was that sense of moral danger, the implied risk of coming up as corrupt as the crime you were investigating, that made the work interesting. Call it the thrill factor. Not a roller-coaster thrill, it was more like falling in slow motion, a kind of skydiver dream where you keep dropping, getting closer and closer to what you hope will be the truth, and all the time you're falling you have your hand on the cord, waiting until the last possible instant to pop open and yank yourself back up, awake, alive again.

When Truman took his leave he was walking a little taller, as if absorbing some of the unpleasant behavioral patterns of the people he wanted to write about had added to his stature. When I shut and bolted the door behind him I was thinking that I liked him quite a lot. He was no longer the laconic nebbish who took notes in Gregg and spoke in monosyllables, he was a priest/reporter pursuing the sacrament of truth.

It must have been that second bourbon.

Chapter Sixteen

Gerald Sutcliffe was sunning himself in a reclining canvas chair on the beach side of the family bath house, which had been converted into a rental cottage some years before. Gerald wasn't wearing his sister's dress this time. He wasn't wearing anything at all.

I had rung the bell for a while but, getting no response, had come around the corner of the vine-covered, gray-shingled building, pushed open a lattice gate, and walked down a wooden walkway that spanned the sand dunes.

"Goodness," said Gerald without opening his eyes. "How embarrassing. I hope that's you, Vanessa, or I shall turn pink all over."

"You're pink already," I told him. "And I'm not Vanessa."

It was September and the southern coast of Maine was getting the heat that had not come in a cool and rainy August. There were striped canvas wind barriers delineating the forty yards or so of beach that belonged to the cottage, and they flopped lazily in the thick air. Gerald shaded his eyes with his hands and squinted at me. He made no move to cover himself.

"I know the voice," he said. "I'm afraid I've burned out my retinas. You know, like Little Orphan Annie? Just little black holes in my head."

He swung his lean legs over the side of the canvas recliner and sat up. His expression was so bemused and mischievous that he made me laugh out loud.

"That's it! It's Connie Kale!"

Before I could do a thing about it he was standing up and embracing me, smelling of coconut oil and salt water.

"Gerald. You're naked."

He stepped back and looked down at himself, feigning surprise. "How *disgusting*. But Constance, dear, don't pretend you're shocked by my poor little thing. I simply lack the dimensions for psychic trauma."

He picked up a beach towel, sighed, and cinched it around his waist. Gerald had the profile of a Barrymore and, luckily for him, had been spared the prodigious O'Hare jaw, which would have spoiled his looks. He came out ahead on one other family trait by inheriting the O'Hare charm without their cunning. Perhaps that is why I had always liked him and managed to overlook his outrageous affectations, which he above all others knew were absurd and comical.

"Have you moved down here?" I asked. "Did Vanessa kick you out of the big house?"

"She wouldn't dare. No, I just come down here to use the beach. Or abuse it, actually."

I asked him if he minded answering a couple of questions. The idea delighted him. He shooed me into a seat under a big beach umbrella and proceeded to arrange himself opposite me, his face tilted up into the sun.

"I'm ready, dear. Proceed with your interrogation. No need to threaten torture, I'm weak and will tell all. I think it's *so* exciting, your being a private eye. I always saw you as a Lauren Bacall type."

No one had ever accused me of resembling Lauren Bacall. I found the comparison typical of Gerald, who had an uncanny talent for seeing you as you wanted to be seen, as the image all of us carry around on our inner mirrors. And as part of the bargain his friends tried to see Gerald as his not-so-secret self-image, that of a young George Sanders playing Dorian Gray, which sometimes blurred into Michael Redgrave in the title role of Oscar Wilde's *The Importance of Being Earnest.*

The overwhelming impression was that Gerald was *très* gay. It was a purposely false impression because despite the cross-dressing and not-dressing Gerald was not actually homosexual. He was just weird.

"I expect you've been giving Papa Doc a hard time? 'Nessa is hoping you'll have him arrested on some spurious charge and thrown into a dungeon."

Papa Doc was his father, Dr. Sutcliffe. The good doctor, who had married late, had very little in common with his two children. As far as I knew there was no open animosity or tension; and likewise there was little affection. I was prejudiced, of course. I couldn't imagine anyone having much affection for Sutcliffe and had always considered it a miracle that neither Gerald nor his sister Vanessa resembled him in the slightest. It was still too early to know whether they would end up resembling their mother Louise, who had been a pitiful, gin-soaked beauty who slid into a severe depression in her mid-forties and did not escape it until she strapped on lead weights and stepped into the pool. Gerald had been about seven years old when it happened, and a real momma's boy except the momma he had attached himself to was their governess. A good thing, considering what happened.

"It's not your father," I told him. "It's Joe Palowski."

Gerald made bug eyes at me and then grinned. His

teeth were as white as Ivory soap. "Joe? Is that his real name? But it seems so *ordinary*. Joe Six Pack, Joe Stripper . . . well, Connie, you just missed him. 'Nessa drove him in to the bus station. He's going up to Portland for the day to visit mommie dearest."

"And he's renting this place from you?"

Gerald had turned his head at the sound of a wave breaking. The tide was running in and big combers were spilling themselves at the feet of the sand dunes. The light came through the water just as each wave broke, green and emerald clear.

"Put it this way. 'Nessa and I are letting poor Randy stay here for a while. We don't actually rent it out because tenants might resist the idea of me lying out here in my birthday suit and I *must* have my sunshine, Connie, or I begin to wilt."

I got the impression that Gerald was willing to answer any questions, providing that I was willing to drag it out of him by formulating clever repartee. Something out of the screenplays he collected. I wasn't sure I was up to it, but determined to give it a whirl for old times' sake.

I took a pair of dark glasses out of my purse and perched them on the end of my nose, looking at him coolly over the rims. That broke him up.

"Oh this is going to be *fun*," he said, laughing. "I do wish I had some secrets to conceal. But you already know the beast in me."

I twirled the sunglasses in my fingers and tried to lower my voice to the fruity contralto of Lauren Bacall.

"Gerald, darling, you *must* tell me how long you've known this Randy person. *Dates*, lovebird, give me times and places and dates."

Gerald was delighted. "Now that's not half bad, Connie. Have you ever thought about the community theater? I have a certain amount of influence at the playhouse. That is, 'Nessa and I give them heaps of money and they pretend to listen to me. I think it would be just too precious if you'd come in for a cattle call. And knock them all dead, of course."

Just too precious was exactly my sentiment. I returned the sunglasses to my purse and gave up the play acting.

"Seriously, Gerald. Tell me about Randy. What he's doing here? How do you happen to know him? What's his connection to Mandy?"

Another big comber exploded. As it collapsed it dragged away parts of the sand dune. The next tide would hurl the sand up somewhere else, and I had the eerie thought that we were floating on the edge of the earth, about to have the ground swept out from under us.

"Of course. I thought you'd never ask. Kitty asked us if we'd let him crash here for a few weeks. He's really quite an interesting fellow and can stay here indefinitely as far as we're concerned. Now what was the rest of the question? Oh, yes, his connection to Mandy. I'm a little vague on that but my impression is that Mandy and Kitty picked him up at some dreadful club in Portland. A country-western sort of place, you know? Actually they were more interested in that other man, the one who was stabbed."

"Jon Maxfield?"

"Mmm. The very one. I never met the man, but Mandy was in raptures over him. I think she brought him up here for a party, but I didn't go because you know I *never* go to parties unless they're my own. Speaking of which we're having one tonight. It's a costume party. All our parties are costume so that Gerald can dress up, you know? You really ought to come, Connie. You can spy on everyone and I'll try and see that a few clues are strewn about."

I ignored the invitation, for the moment, and tried to steer him back on track. "Maxfield, Gerald. Was he a dope connection? And how does Randy fit in?"

"My dear, *everyone* is a dope connection these days.

Actually, I don't do the stuff myself because it wreaks havoc with the sinus and I *do* hate to sneeze."

"And Randy?"

"I'm not really sure what Randy's attitude is toward sneezing. It wouldn't surprise me at all if he used every single orifice, if you know what I mean, dear, and I suppose that includes the nostrils. But I *don't* really think he's selling any great quantity of the stuff, or there would be more of those snuffed-out zombies hanging about here. And it has been very *very* quiet. You're the first visitor I've seen down here in, oh, *eons*."

When I got up to leave, the striped canvas wind barriers had become translucent with salt spray and the tide, having done its worst, was starting to back away. Gerald stood up with me.

"Don't forget us, sweets. The party? *Please* come. We shall be devastated if you don't see us in costume."

Gerald raised his lithe arms to gesture. The towel dropped, as if on cue. I think he'd been rehearsing.

Win Browning was sitting on the clubhouse steps. In addition to being a natural smiler he is also a professional smiler, grinning at hacks and slices and duck hooks and all the various afflictions of the game he teaches, and as a result his eyes are pale and sunbleached and surrounded by a network of fine wrinkles. He wears a pencil-thin mustache that might have been borrowed from Don Ameche and when he walks he strolls with the rolling gait of Popeye the Sailor, with his toes dinged in. I've known him forever and he treats me like he did when I was five years old—as an adult. September was one of the club's busiest times of year, what with a couple of tournaments and a spate of fall guests up to combine golf and foliage, which mostly involved looking for lost balls under piles of yellow oak leaves. So I had called to make an appointment to see him and he had insisted that we make it a playing date.

125

"Hire me out for nine," he had teased. "And put it on the Governor's tab."

I'd agreed to pay the teaching fee and neglected to tell him it wouldn't be billed to Alfred O'Hare. This was strictly for my own satisfaction. To be honest it was also an excuse to try out the new set of woods my father had built for me. Naturally I suspected that he had been in touch with Win Browning, hence the "deal" Win made before agreeing to fill me in on the details of Byron's accidental drowning.

He kissed me on the lips, which surprised me.

"Hey, these days I steal whatever I can," he said, laughing. "And I cleaned my dentures, knowing you'd be here."

"You don't have dentures, Win."

"Not yet. I'm practicing."

His electric cart was at the first tee. I asked if he minded walking the nine and he readily assented.

"It was wet this morning, but the sun has burned it off now. There's a new trap on the second you'll hate if you hit it."

There was something stilted in the way he rattled off the usual preround chatter, and it wasn't until I'd set my bag down and extracted a driver that I realized why Win was suddenly nervous. He was trying to distract me from the birds along the rail. Everyone who worked in the clubhouse and several of the members were grouped along the clubhouse porch, trying to pretend they weren't there to watch us tee off.

"Robbie," said Win, clearing his throat self-consciously. "I didn't mention any names, but Robbie saw where I'd penciled you in and passed the word."

Robbie was his assistant. What I wanted to do was tee up a shag ball and drive it right into Robbie's smart little grin. Instead I turned my back to the rail birds and tried to loosen up. It had been four years and I figured I'd be lucky to make contact. I was right. The ball carried about two hundred yards before veering off into the rough on the right side of the fairway. But the audience couldn't see that from where they were and for all they knew the drive had carried two eighty to the stake. So it could have been worse.

"I wish you'd have duffed it," Win confided as we shouldered our bags. "We don't have much to talk about around here now. That would have lasted through the winter."

Byron O'Hare had done a beautiful job of laying out the Sankaty Head course. It had the narrow majesty and towering oaks of a club made in the previous century. With the twists and turns and the green coverage, you were hardly aware of the two hundred or so homes that bordered the course and were its reason for being. Partly my affection has to do with learning how to play there, and partly it is a loyalty spawned in childhood, when every blade of grass came under my father's scrutiny.

Browning has a nice compact swing. I've seen him place a bushel basket two hundred and sixty yards away, drive a bucket of balls at it and not miss any of them by more than ten or fifteen yards. So we parted company at the rough and I waded in with a five-iron. I watched him hit a four-wood, placing the ball right down the middle between the bunkers, an easy nine to the green. Meanwhile I worked my heels into the puckerbrush, told myself not to swing too hard, and swung too hard anyway. The ball skittered out onto the fairway, just barely.

I wanted to pick up my ball and go home, but Win was waving me on.

"Relax, Connie. That last swing looked like something Babe Ruth cooked up after three quick whiskeys. Why not try that pretty new three-wood that old buzzard whittled for you?"

Why not indeed. With nothing to lose I settled in over

the ball and thought about the first green. When I had completed my follow-through something clicked. It had felt good.

"Where's the ball, Win?"

"Don't jiggle my whiskers, young lady. It's on the green about ten feet shy of the hole, right where you knew it would be."

Oddly enough, he was right. I *had* known it would be there. Anyone who tells you golf isn't a game you play in your head has probably been lobotomized. They say you never forget how to ride a bicycle once you've learned; I can vouch the same for the game of golf, which it seemed I couldn't quite erase no matter how hard I'd tried. Naturally, after making one good shot I bought right back into it and approaching the green I could feel a lump in my throat and icy ball bearings sloshing around in my innards.

Browning had popped a nine-iron about the same distance from the pin. We were even.

"Uh, I think I'm closer, Win."

"You're right. I just put my micrometer on it and you're at least a millimeter closer."

It wasn't a serious protest. Win played this hole several times a day in the course of his lessons. For an eagle putt he might have gotten serious, not for a mere par. Not that it was mere to me. I watched him take his stance and then knock it into the cup without even pausing to take a breath.

"Looks easy the way you do it."

"More fun watching you," he rejoined. "Better hands and better legs."

I was wearing a pair of white walking shorts, old ones that were a little too short, from repeated washings, and he made me self-conscious. I stood over the ball too long and had to back away.

"Isn't this dumb?" I said. "I quit this game already, what difference does it make if I drop this putt?"

What difference, indeed. I'd missed the last crucial

putt, that killer in Atlanta, and four years had passed since I decided not to dust myself off and climb back on the horse again. Suddenly it was important to cancel that bad memory by holing my first putt.

The stroke was all wrong, but it was too late to call back the ball. It wobbled along the short nap, looking somehow drunken and lost, and I was astonished when it curled to the left and disappeared. Plop.

Win nodded and was wise enough to refrain from patting me on the back. After that it was all right. I made some good shots and some bad shots and was enjoying the stroll around nine, my thoughts entirely occupied with the small adjustments and decisions of the game.

By the time we'd crossed the creek bridge and rounded up the seventh I'd completely forgotten my original purpose. It was Browning who reminded me.

"It was right around this time of year," he said before teeing up his ball. "But foggy as hell. We'd been having hot weather and the beaches were packed and then the air temperature dropped about ten degrees and the steam just started rolling in off the beaches. You've seen it like that before."

I sure had. On days like that the sky could be clear right over your head and yet all around you the white mist was thick, shrinking the world into one small green circle, sometimes no bigger in diameter than how far you might hit a pitching wedge. It was like being snowblinded and sometimes it could be frightening, when something like a bare tree branch loomed out of the mist, or a man remained faceless, until you got close enough to touch him.

"Your dad had me out clipping the fringe. I'd adjusted the blades, but this was still in the days of big push mowers and it was hot, muggy work. I was soaked to the knees. Funny how you can remember little details like that. Ask me what I did this time last week and I'd probably draw a blank. But the day Byron O'Hare died, that I remember like yesterday."

The seven was a fairly long par three. Browning could hit the ball farther than I could, but it was still a difficult green to drive if the ball didn't carry perfectly. It didn't. He was in the bunker and I saw him looking ruefully at his three-iron.

"I don't know what there is about this hole . . ." He was shaking his head. Although my own shot wasn't bad, it hadn't carried forward and was about twenty feet into the fringe to the left of the green. At least I hadn't let Byron's ghost grab the ball and hook me into the pond.

"Anyhow, there weren't too many parties out that day. Hell, the clubhouse, the old one, was fogged in solid. Couldn't see the parking lot. Then again Byron hadn't left from the first tee. He almost never did."

I asked him why that was.

"There," he said, pointing with a club. "See that stone wall to the right of the bunker? It's overgrown now, but there used to be a path that went right up to the O'Hare estate. Byron had cut it in himself, just so he could pop out the back door and walk through a few holes whenever the mood hit him. It's unfortunate you never got to know the man. He was a helluva good guy. I mean, take a look around you, the man was an artist."

I nodded in agreement and didn't bother telling Win that when I'd looked at aerial shots of O'Hare golf courses I'd been looking for huge dollar signs carved into the earth.

"Usually he just played seven, eight, and nine. He was a pretty fair golfer, too. Light years better than his brother or Pudge. Sometimes he'd tell me to leave the mower or the clippers or whatever I was doing and play along with him. Let me use the clubs right out of his bag. *That* tells you something about Byron O'Hare. Imagine the Governor loaning anyone a putter even? Or a dime to mark the ball? Hell, it was Byron who encouraged me. Said he knew folks down at the qualifying school and when I had my game together he'd set things up for me to try qualifying. Even made sure your dad gave me a raise so I could save up the money."

The memories were visibly exciting Browning as we came up to our second shots. He hit his wedge so hard that his shot carried all the way across the green and into the fringe again.

"I *never* do that. That must be Byron, giving me a nudge."

With his example to guide me I very carefully chipped up close to the pin. An "easy" three-footer. Win suggested we sit down for a few minutes before finishing out the hole. There was no one behind us; I suspected he had told Robbie to hold back any parties until we had a good head start. He knew I didn't want hurrying that day.

We sat on our bags, gazing into Byron's pond. The water was still and I could see clouds reflected there, moving across the blue sky.

". . . what happened was, I ran out of gas," Browning was saying. He wasn't looking at me when he recalled the day, he was staring at an angle off toward the high bunker. Looking into the past. "That mower made a racket, you know. So then suddenly she coughed out and it got quiet. Fine with me, I was soaking wet and my arms were tired and I needed a break. So I wasn't thinking about going for another can of gas immediately. In those days I smoked, and I remember lighting up a Lucky and trying to convince myself it wasn't burning my throat up. That's when I heard that funny sound."

He gave the phrase a peculiar emphasis: *that funny sound*.

"I guess I'd call it a moaning. At the time I thought maybe a seagull had run into a telephone pole and broken its neck and was dying, because it was that kind of sound. Like something couldn't get its breath."

I was listening and I could hear it, too, almost. I was surprised at the intensity of Browning's recollection and understood why my father had sent me to him. He remembered everything, the sounds and the smells and the touch of damp fog on his unbristled cheeks.

"That went on for I don't know, maybe half a minute. The next thing I hear is a tractor starting up. I mean that's what it sounded like—you know what the fog can do to sounds. What it was was one of the old gas-powered carts we had in those days. It starts coming my way, from the sound of it; I don't know what made me do it, but I called out. I shouted. And the cart veered towards me. It was Pudge. He was crying, sobbing. I know that's hard for you to believe, knowing what a control type guy he is, but that day he was crying. So that funny sound must have been him sobbing."

I thought it was odd how convinced everyone seemed to be of Pudge's stout exterior. Not that I think there is anything wrong with a man crying when the situation calls for tears.

"I finally figure out what he is trying to say is that Byron is in the pond. I was confused—what pond? The water hazard was even shallower back then than it is now. At most three feet. But I'm running along, slipping on the wet grass—that hysteria of Pudge's was damned infectious, let me tell you—and then the pond looms up out of the fog and that is when I see Byron. At first I couldn't focus, you know? Like one of those pictures where objects are camouflaged in a kind of a busy background?"

Browning's tight curls of hair were mostly gray now, but his gestures and articulation were as animate as if he were still a boy of seventeen. I got the impression that after all these years he was still working something out in his mind.

"It looked like a shirt, all swelled up with air, kind of floating up among the bullrushes, which there were more of back then. Then I saw the arms and just his fingertips breaking the surface of the water. He was right next to the shore, not two feet from the bank. That's what I can't understand about it. I mean why the hell didn't Pudge just pull him out of the water? Why did he panic like that?"

I asked him how Byron had fallen into the pond. That was the question I had wanted answered when I originally made the appointment to talk with Browning.

"They never knew. Pudge said he was on the other side of the green, trying to find his ball in the sandtrap. Which I can believe, since the guy was *always* hitting that trap. When he came up over the top he didn't see Byron anywhere. So he played out the hole—I guess maybe he thought his uncle nipped into the woods to, ah, relieve himself. Finally he saw the body floating there and that's what freaked him out. At the inquest they said that Byron had probably had some kind of seizure and fallen backward into the water. It only takes about thirty seconds to drown if you're unconscious, or if your lungs fill. I think Pudge was pretty ashamed of himself—I mean what if Byron *wasn't* dead when he first saw him there? Anyhow, Pudge was out of circulation for about a month. Never even went to the funeral. . . ."

I asked him where the Governor was during the aftermath of the tragedy. He gave me a funny look.

"He really *was* the Governor then. He was running for reelection. That was the primary he lost, you know. Really the beginning of the end of his political career. And I always wondered if maybe he didn't blame Pudge a little."

I asked why the Governor would blame his son for that.

"The bad publicity. The old man was convinced that the bad press about Byron's death lost him the election. They made quite a fuss about it at the inquest hearings, you know. About it being a peculiar kind of accident. Like maybe someone was to blame."

I thought about Nesmith, the coroner, and the cool, moist touch of his hands. It made me shudder a little, in recollection. I wondered if Nesmith had been the one to raise the questions, or if he had been the one to answer them and thus settle the case. Recalling the Governor's reaction to his name I thought the former more likely.

"Let's make it interesting," said Browning as we went back to the green to finish the hole. "Let's play for cokes."

The mood was broken. And as it turned out we both took bogeys on the seventh. I decided to blame it on the ghost of Byron O'Hare.

Chapter Seventeen

It took a little while, but I finally named that tune. It was Bach's *Toccata and Fugue* in some key or other, an organ solo familiar to us nonclassicists because Walt Disney had it reorchestrated for *Fantasia*. I had parked my rental Chevy in the road in case an early departure became necessary. As I trudged up the gravel driveway toward the Sutcliffe estate, checking out the strange mixture of cars that ranged in distinction from Mercedes sedans to beat-up VW bugs, Bach gave way to The Talking Heads.

"That would be Gerald," I said aloud. There were other guests heading for both the main and side entrances, and no one paid me any heed. There was a quickness in their steps that implied a willingness to quaff free liquor and a pre-party anxiety about how long the bar would be open.

I hadn't known how to dress. Should I dye my hair purple? Wrap myself in aluminum foil? Rouge my nipples? The dilemma was resolved by squeezing into a well-worn pair of blue jeans and a reasonably presentable satin blouse. In a mood of total abandon I painted my toenails and wore open sandals. As near as I could remember the last time I'd painted my toenails was for the junior prom, the one when my date didn't show. Maybe he just couldn't face my bare feet.

Several yellow spots spilled light out over the grounds. Through the big windows, some of which were thrown open to the unseasonably warm night, I could see that the party was already cranked up and rolling. I stood in the yard, smelling the scent of flowers and fresh-mown grass as I watched the people mixing and dancing, until a flick of voyeuristic guilt forced me inside.

My first impression, after snagging a drink from the help-yourself bar that had been set up in the sprawling formal dining room, was one of surprise that Gerald and Vanessa knew so many people I did not know. Nor was the gathering as immediately decadent as I had imagined—hoped—it might be. Which is not to say there wasn't plenty of purple and pink hair and translucent blouses, and a few leather upholstered couples, seemingly zippered together at the hips.

"I'd know you anywhere," said a young man with slightly pocked cheeks and luminescent blue eyes. "You're Tracy Kent, of the Atwater Kents."

I tuned him out. He didn't seem the least put off, and I heard him trying the same line on someone who resembled me (and Tracy, supposedly) not in the slightest. Maybe there was a handbook circulating the Head on how-to-pick-up-girls-by-mistaking-them-for-rich-debs.

"Maidstone," which is the old, formal name for the estate now occupied by the Sutcliffes, is adjacent to the O'Hares', and was built in the same era. It has the same high ceilings designed to waft away the blue cigar smoke of industrial magnates, the overscale, multipaned windows meant to keep a brigade of maids busy with vinegar and

Bon Ami, the double kitchen and restaurant-style pantries. In addition to the wing that houses the bedroom suites, there are four ballroom-sized rooms on the ground floor, all of which open onto a two-storied central hallway with the obligatory grand staircase, which was wide enough to walk a pony up sideways.

I knew that for a fact because Vanessa had done just that one summer, while attempting to train a rather dim-witted beast to tap dance, just like Francis the Mule in the movies. That little exercise in animal husbandry was canceled when Dr. Sutcliffe, robed and barefoot on his way to breakfast, stepped on a horsebun and noticed hoofprints in the Oriental runner.

I wasn't around to hear him, but could well imagine his dark, Dickensian threats about sending it to the glue factory. Maybe that explained Vanessa's fantasy of casting the old boy into a dungeon, although probably it had more to do with the two children having inherited their mother's estate, while the good doctor, a blue blood but unmonied in his own right, was forced to suck up to his brother-in-law, the former Governor.

"Darling, I am thrilled and amazed! You *came!*"

It was an entrance worthy of Loretta Young, or maybe Mae West on her way down from the bordello. I had squeezed my way through the crowd and into the big marble foyer under the staircase. Gerald was coming down and stopped to pose on the third step, looking as chic and elegant as it is possible for a boy to look who is wearing his sister's taffeta gown.

"'Nessa, look who's here," said Gerald, turning to his sister, who was dressed rather conservatively in a veldt-green chamois skirt and leotard. She was as long-legged as the pony that had failed to navigate the staircase and still exuded that air of intelligent haughtiness I remembered as a child. She had pinned a diamond and pearl brooch between her breasts, doubtless an heirloom from Louise.

Vanessa gave me a smooch without much feeling to it. We'd never been closer than mutual tolerance. "Gerald told me you were down at the cottage. Is Randy in some kind of trouble?"

Gerald grinned, showing off his lipstick, making no pretense about not listening in while his sister grilled me.

I told her, truthfully, that I didn't know.

"I hardly know the man," she said levelly, fixing me with her astonishing green eyes, emerald clear and slightly devious. "We let him stay as a favor to Kitty. We felt we owed it to her."

Vanessa was an exception to the third generation rule observed by so many of her Head contemporaries: Go Thou Forth With Trust Funds Into The World and Consume Vast Quantities Of Drugs. For all I knew Vanessa *did* do vast quantities of drugs (although the clear green eyes belied that) but it had not prevented her from taking an advanced degree in cybernetics, nor in forming a consulting firm, reputedly a big money maker, whose function it was to advise computer manufacturers of the latest trendy gadgets soon to be in vogue. Nor did Vanessa appear to suffer from that other third-generational disease: Thou Shalt Go Forth With Inheritance And Disperse To The Deserving. By that I mean 'Nessa didn't concern herself with such grim and tawdry charitable causes as world hunger, or environmentalism, or concerns over the proliferation of nuclear weapons. As a matter of fact I had an idea that the lovely sister of wacky and neo-radical Gerald supplemented her income by doing research for the same conservative lobbyists who had once supported her great-uncle Alfred.

"I was just doing a background investigation," I assured her. "If Randy has a warrant outstanding you'll be the first to know."

We traded smiles only slightly cooler than an arctic spring.

With a plastic drink cup held before me like a chalice, I steered through the first floor. I estimated that less than half of the two hundred or so guests had followed Gerald's suggestion and come in costume other than what they wore habitually, be it leather or lace, levi or vinyl. I did see two different people got up as plastic bottles of Hunt's ketchup. I wasn't able to determine if they'd come as a pair or just had similar taste in condiments.

In one of the back halls I came upon a rather morose-looking gentleman. He was leaning against a wall and studying his empty glass. He wore an artist's full beard and was dressed in a way that I thought looked normal for a man in his early forties. That is, a tweed sports jacket with a loosely knotted tie, whipcord trousers, and for Indian summer chic, a pair of beige espadrilles. He looked safe enough and I asked him why so many in the crowd were wearing dark glasses.

"You noticed?" he said, not brightening in the slightest. "Well, if you had to look into their eyes, you'd know."

"Really? What would I see there?"

He snorted and shook his shaggy head. "Despair. Greed. Suburban malaise. Existential nonbeing. And also something infinitely worse," he confided. "*Youth.*"

I asked him if he was an artist.

"Don't be ridiculous," he said, as if insulted. "I'm Vanessa Sutcliffe's broker. I handle her finances."

"Maybe you should run away to Tahiti," I suggested. "Like Gauguin."

He turned away, shutting me out. That's part of my charm, the ability to offend total strangers in ten words or less. I headed back to the bar for a refill. The music booming in the parqueted ballroom was a far cry (and a loud

139

one) from the Strauss waltzes in favor when the mansion was designed. I saw two Coneheads pogoing, and a couple of people got up as scantily clad space vampires. Looking a little out of context, three people dressed as members of a motorcycle gang were hogging space at the bar. On closer examination their prison tattoos revealed them to be the genuine article. Stiff whiskers sprouting from a pasty face leered at me, "Hey honey. Wanna ride my hog? Baby, I *guarantee* it was made in America."

His companions of the highway were chuckling like demented kewpie dolls. I knew better than to trade one-liners with potential gang rapists and as I turned with my freshened drink I bumped into a slender blond attired as a tennis pro, wearing practice whites and carrying a racket.

"Hi, Connie."

"Oh. Hello, Tommy." I could see myself in his mirrored sunglasses. "I didn't recognize you behind the bug eyes."

"That's my costume."

True enough. The tennis whites were what he wore to work each day at the Sankaty Tennis Club, where he was very popular with the ladies. Which is probably the reason I had married him and definitely the reason we divorced.

"Is this business or pleasure?" he asked, standing a little closer than was comfortable.

"A little of each." I was looking for an out. Standing around and trading clichés with a former spouse is not my idea of a good time. I drained the cup of booze, trying to convince myself that the constriction in the area of my heart was a result of the thumping bass. The music swelled, making the air seem syrupy thick, and he moved even closer.

"Lookit those two," he half shouted, gesturing toward the crowded dance floor with his racket. "Maybe I have a lot of nerve, but those guys are disgusting."

Swirling colored lights had been switched on and it was hard to distinguish individuals in the writhing mass. Gradually I was able to focus on the two who had offended the professional tennis bum whose free hand had somehow found its way to the small of my back.

Kitty was wearing an electric blue skirt that was slit about an inch beyond up-to-here. Her tiny halter top straps were strategically loose, as was her head, which was rolling around on her tanned shoulders like a brunette ball bearing. Bo Bernardi, dressed as I'd seen him at the Birmingham, barechested and wearing hip tight designer jeans, was rolling his head the same way. I don't know what they called the dance they were doing, but "Guillotine" describes it.

They were both higher than stratus clouds, if pupils dilated to pinpoints are any indication. Bo had his thumbs tucked into the waist of his jeans and was dancing just a little off the beat, as if he were hearing the music a split second late. As I watched, Kitty hiked her skirt up around her waist and did a kind of limbo rock, her slender, sun-buttered thighs tensing until she and Bo were pelvis to pelvis, moving together.

"See what I mean?" said my biggest mistake. "No class. I guess they deserve each other."

"It's young love, Tommy."

He grimaced at the diminutive use of his name. I was being mean; only his mother called him "Tommy" and he didn't love her, either.

The hand on my lower back became insistent, working itself under my blouse.

"Whatsa matter, Tommy? Not enough action at the tennis club? No debutante fannies to paddle with the great big racket of yours?"

The music hit a low spot just then and I found myself shouting. Tom backed away, scowling and embarrassed.

The three drunken bikers, who were beginning to look like creatures out of the bar scene in *Star Wars*, made hooting comments about who they would like to paddle, and with what.

"For Christ's sake," Tom hissed. "It's been four years. Can't you forgive and forget?"

See what I mean about trading clichés with a former spouse? No matter how real the situation might have once been, it inevitably degenerates into dialogue from an afternoon soap. I made a quick apology, patted him on the butt to restore his ego, and made myself scarce. As I brushed by Kitty and Bo they disentangled themselves momentarily and mustered up pinpoint glares that let me know they knew I was spying on them.

I needed air and solitude. The mansion had a screened-in porch and I found one corner of it, overlooking the cliffs, which had not been taken over by necking couples. Fishing out a cigarette, I wondered if it was the dumb little scene with Tom that made me feel so low, or if the whole investigation was giving me a psychic hangover. The three strippers, the two sisters, and the Portland connection just didn't seem to fit into an equation that equaled ten thousand dollars in a corpse's pocket.

"Connie, my dear, you're supposed to be out there mingling and picking up *clues*."

I jumped. Gerald was sitting in the dark, swinging on a well-oiled glider. In the shadows he looked very much like a girl, and that may have been why he was posing there. He had pronounced the word "clue" with an intonation he must have picked up from the BBC Masterpiece Theater.

"If you must know, I've been waiting for you to seek me out, dear. To confront me, you know, with my little secret."

The voice was pose and affectation, and something else: an edge of fear, or maybe a plea for forgiveness. I sat down next to Gerald and tried not to smile when his sister's gown rustled.

"I thought maybe my father told you," he said in his real voice. "About what happened with Mandy and me."

This was going to be a confession and the darkness was the screen between us. All I lacked was the ability to give absolution.

"I thought *everyone* knew about us," said Gerald. His voice gained tension and his figure became quite still. "It was years ago, but the old man still looks at me like I'm some kind of infected scab, or a boil he's dying to lance."

He told me it happened the summer that both he and Mandy turned fourteen. I could remember that year, and how wild and uncontrollable Mandy had been. Puberty was like a drug to her and she had cultivated jealous teenage crushes between herself and half a dozen surfer boys, most of them several years older than herself. She'd told me about the abortion a couple of years later, and I'd always assumed that one of the beach boys was responsible.

"Oh, she loved to talk about it," Gerald was saying. "Almost every evening she'd come up to my room and tell me all about what she'd been doing on the beach. Teasing the boys. Touching them. Flirting outrageously and using that dirty mouth of hers." He giggled and touched my arm with a hand that was icy and dry. "I mean *swearing,* dear. Fellatio came a few years later. Anyhow, she thought she was a regular Dragon Lady, playing those poor dumb surfer boys off against each other. It was like girl-talk between us. Except that I wasn't a girl."

From the bushes near the railing came the unmistakable sound of a couple in heat. We both pretended to ignore the muted cries and whispers. Had Gerald written his confession as a screenplay, he might well have cued in the comic soundtrack, a tragedy of manners under the summer porch.

143

"One evening she appeared holding this reefer. Holding it in both hands like an offering. One of the surfer boys had given it to her—get Mandy stoned and then off with her knickers and into paradise. Well, she tricked him out of the dope and brought it to me. Naturally, I was curious. I'd never even seen an actual joint before. And for Mandy it was kind of an instructional thing: let's teach Gerald how to get high.

"I just about coughed my little lungs up, trying to hold the smoke down. At first, nothing but this sicky type feeling. Then the bedroom started to change, you know? The walls expanded and the ceiling became a kind of sky above us and we were both floating on this *cloud*. Of course it was only my bed, but it seemed very much like a cloud." He paused, not looking at me. What I could see of his rouged smile was grim and uncertain. "And then Mandy goes: *let's feel the air against our bodies. It'll be like floating in syrup.* Isn't that an odd image, floating in syrup? I was so high I didn't know what she meant until she stripped her clothes off. And then of course I had to take mine off, too, or I would spoil the mood. It was all very electric, all very exciting. It made me feel I was closer to Mandy than I'd ever been to any person, even 'Nessa . . ."

Gerald's voice was fading and I had to lean forward. In the dim light I could see his mascara running.

"I swear to you, Connie, I didn't even know what sex was. When I heard other boys describe fucking I thought they must be joking. Put *your* thing inside *her* thing? It just seemed too ridiculous to be real. Why would anybody want to do that? But I found out why. Mandy showed me."

I was enough of an amateur psychologist to wonder if Mandy's seduction had anything to do with Gerald's penchant for dressing up in his sister's clothes. Just formulating the question made me feel a little creepy, so I kept it to myself.

"It was a long time before I realized what she'd been doing that day," said Gerald. His voice had another edge to it this time; one of resentment and as much anger as he was capable of mustering. "She used me. Mandy was good at using people. She wanted to screw around with all those surfer boys and she didn't want to be a virgin, so she impaled herself on nice little Gerald, who was convenient and too frightened to tell anyone about it, not even 'Nessa. And then when Mandy got preggie, Gerald was still there to point the finger at. And even more convenient was the fact that Gerald's father was a doctor. *Now* do you get it, Connie? Have I dropped enough clues?"

Gerald took the cigarette out of my hand and began to puff it furiously. Yes, I thought, it was handy indeed that Dr. Sutcliffe had married into the O'Hare family, where, for a price, he was able to dispense drugs and abort the mystery fetuses of naughty teenage girls. It was a sordid little story out of the past, but I could not see where it connected to the sordid little murder I was investigating in the present.

"Gerald," I said, "have you ever talked to anyone about this? I mean professionally?"

He laughed and handed the glowing stub of the cigarette back. "Only twice a week. Tuesdays and Thursdays. Look, dear, don't worry about me. If I didn't have this to mess me up it would just be something else. I'm the type."

He used a piece of tissue paper to blot the mascara, stood up on his high heels (which he handled better than I ever did) and went back into the noise. I flicked the cigarette butt against the screen, thought better of it, and put the stub in an ashtray. Best not to leave anything smoldering in this house, however insignificant. I imagined the whole place bursting into flame one day, spontaneously combusted by the heat of bitter memories.

I was surprised to find the central hallway relatively

empty. Little Bo Peep was passed out on the landing, smelling of fruit and rum, but most of the witches and warlocks and pseudo film stars were crowded into the ballroom. I caught a glimpse of the reason as I walked by. Randy the Rogue, down to a microscopic G-string, was strutting his stuff. No one was trying to stuff dollar bills into his pouch, not that he seemed to mind. I wondered how he was getting paid, and by whom.

Someone came up behind me and I turned a little too quickly. "I'm going to do it," said the stockbroker with the Gauguin beard. "I'm going to do like you said. I'm going to give it all up and go away. Not Tahiti, but maybe Antigua. Does that sound okay, Antigua?"

He looked feverish and slightly drunk. I thought he was putting me on, but his expression was in dead earnest. He tugged at the sleeve of my blouse and whispered fiercely. "You come too. We'll start over. We'll be born again."

"What about your job?" I said, backing toward the door. He looked crazier than the Ancient Mariner. "What about taking care of Vanessa's money?"

"*Screw* Vanessa! Screw all of these creeps."

"You're probably the only one who hasn't." He was watching my lips, but I don't think he heard a word I said. "Good luck in Antigua."

I ditched him there, as he muttered about tropical paradise and love under the palms. I was headed down the curving driveway, taking deep lungfuls of sea-moistened air, when a shadow passed in front of the moon. The shadow moved forward, into a slice of the outside floodlights, and a giant in tangerine overalls glided by.

Had someone spiked the punch? Evidently it was no hallucination, because when I looked again Doctor Nervo was still there, his bulk receding as he walked briskly up the driveway and into the light streaming from the portico.

There were cheers and whistles from inside and I assumed that Randy had dropped his leaf just as the giant entered.

There was a static pulse in my tired brain that said: follow the big man inside and ask him why he isn't behind his horseshoe bar at prime time on Saturday night. Then he would tell me a tale, or put the "Super Python" on me, and I'd wrestled with too many lies in the last few days to face him again.

The radio in the rental Chevy wasn't bad. One of the local stations was caught in a forties time warp, and I let Hoagy Carmichael drive me home, whistling a version of "Star Dust" he'd written just for me.

Chapter Eighteen

The door was unlocked when I got home. I am not in the habit of leaving it that way, so I stood there on the front porch, key in hand. What I wanted in my hand was the .32 caliber pistol I keep locked in my file cabinet. I should have filed it under *D* for dumb; a lot of good it was doing me there. And if whoever had jimmied my lock had found it . . . it was enough to make me want to join the N.R.A. and take the pledge to wear my God-given weapon in a holster, cowboy style.

I pushed the door open and thought I'd never seen an interior quite so dark. A vortex of shadows and imagined shapes from childhood nightmares. From out of the vortex came a sound. Someone was whistling the theme to "Teddy Bears' Picnic"!

If you go out in the woods today you're in for a big surprise. I stepped inside and reached for the light switch. At first glance nothing obvious had been disturbed. The door to my bedroom was standing open and I could see naked feet protruding over the edge of the mattress.

"Richard, you scared me to death."

He was lying on the bed, his head propped up on the pillows, a sweating bottle of Molson Ale balanced on his flat, furry tummy. Some Teddy Bear. "It couldn't have been that bad," he said. "You're still breathing."

"How the hell did you get in here?"

"If you don't want a policeman picking your lock, you shouldn't install a police lock, Connie old sport, old dear. Come here and give us a kiss."

I kicked off my heels and lobbed one at him. He deflected it with the side of his hand, like a boy playing ping pong.

"You're drunk, aren't you?"

"A little," he admitted. "Just a teensy bit."

"Me, too," I said, sitting on the edge of the bed. I had to shove his feet over and when I touched him his toes wriggled. "Just a teensy bit."

"Isn't that a nice coincidence?" he said, handing me the cold bottle. "I like that satin blouse, by the way. Why don't you take it off and hang it up and give it a rest?"

It seemed like a good idea. There was no reason why I should let a naked lieutenant of detectives deter me from disrobing in my own bedroom; that would be a violation of rights. If I gave that up, what would follow?

"I had another violation in mind," said Richard, after hearing me explain my position. "A moving violation."

There is still a law on the books against the crime of adultery in the great state of Maine. After we'd renewed our mutual felony I slipped on a robe and went out to the refrigerator and brought back another bottle of ale to share. I thought it was weak of me to amend my bourbon habit in favor of his ale.

"Hey, save a little of that for me."

"I'm proving that I'm not weak," I said, holding the half-emptied bottle against my hot forehead. "I'm as strong as any man. Want to hear me belch?"

He had that postcoital, puppy dog look in his eyes.

"You're a funny kid, Con. I really wish things were different. I wish I could . . ."

"Skip it, Richard. And tell me what you're really doing here."

He tried to look hurt. "You mean I wasn't really doing it? I thought—"

"Hey, fun is fun. Am I complaining? I just know damn well you've got something cooking in that small cunning brain of yours. So what happened?"

What had happened was that the Sicilian dreamboat was no longer in his cell. He had been bailed out earlier in the evening.

"Wait a minute," I said. Just the thought of the Governor's fury made me shiver a little. No wonder Richard was a teensy bit drunk. "I thought the bond was set at fifty grand?"

It had been set at fifty grand, Richard told me. Which was as much as they could push for on a second-degree murder charge the country prosecutor had very little faith in making stick. Tony Steel, G-string and all, was good for about five hundred dollars, so it had seemed safe enough. Until a four-hundred-pound Goodyear Blimp, painted dayglow orange, had floated in with a paper sack full of cash.

"Doctor Nervo," I said, feeling it start to click into place. "The ex-wrestler. He works for Arnold Maury."

"Yeah. Now wasn't that sweet of those guys? Passing the hat around the bar to make bail for poor little Tony, the tulip toes of the Ranchero Lounge? I mean it does your heart good, knowing there are people out there who care."

We did a little more guzzling and then a little more nuzzling, although both of us were too numbed with alcohol and fatigue to get much out of it by then. Even as we lay entwined, waiting for sleep, we talked in monosyllables about the case. Mixing romance and murder is not a good preliminary for a sound night's sleep, and my dreams were confused and empty.

Before dawn broke I was aware that Richard was up and dressing to leave. When he came over to kiss me on the forehead I feigned sleep—if I'd been awake I might have been tempted to ask him who he was planning to breakfast with.

My own breakfast was very simple indeed. Instant coffee, black. When the caffeine got my heart pumping again I took a long cool shower and tried to see if a lot of soap would wash away a hangover. The experiment was a failure, but I felt clean and cool, if not very alert.

Sunday morning. Most of the women I'd gone to school with had already scrambled the eggs and popped the toast and spooned the goo into Ishcabibel's cute little tooferless mouth. Next on the agenda was a trip to church with the kids in knee socks, or maybe settling down with hubby to fight over who got the funny papers.

Poor devils. *They* weren't fortunate enough to be single and working and sitting over the third cup of powdered coffee, alone and hungover and staring at the telephone. While they had to suffer the indignity of being given Godiva chocolates on Mother's Day, and being taken out for their anniversaries, and having the same old date on New Year's Eve. I mean how many of them had the thrill of being propositioned by a fortyish stockbroker who wants to share his nervous breakdown with you?

I must admit the existential nightmare of suburban matrimony looks pretty good when you've just spent the night with a faithless cop whose idea of whispering sweet nothings is to chat up the fine points of blackmail.

I kept looking at the telephone and the telephone kept looking at me. Eventually the telephone won and I dialed the Governor's number and told him about Tony Steel walking.

"Those sons of bitches," he said. "So they're going to

let a cold-blooded murderer prowl the streets? A damn geek who earns his living exposing himself."

I let him run on for a while, getting it out of his system. The response was that of a rattled, elderly man, out of character for him. Maybe he hadn't had his goat milk. I assured him he would be apprised of any new developments, which seemed to calm him a little.

One down. I opened the book, found Nesmith's number, and dialed. The ringing went on for a good long while. A child answered.

"Could I speak to Dr. Nesmith?"

"Daddy!" The phone dropped with a bang. I could hear the child call, "Nubbaphone for you, Daddy!"

I hadn't pictured Nesmith as having offspring, at least not the human kind. Maybe some sort of exotic bread mold he kept in numbered jars; certainly not a little girl with an affectionate giggle. Shame overcame me until I remembered the pleasure Daddy took when he played at cutting up dead people.

"Dr. Nesmith, this is Connie Kale. I'm sorry to disturb you on a Sunday morning like this, but I was discussing a case with Detective Stein yesterday and he suggested I ask you about the details."

That was only three lies, not bad for the Sabbath. Nesmith seemed enchanted with the idea of conversing with me. I had to assure him that a housecall was not necessary. He gave the impression of a man quite willing to administer a physical, needed or not.

"No no, all I want to do is jog your memory," I said, meaning not your blood pressure, you old corpse lecher. "Thirty years ago."

"But honey, you weren't even *born* thirty years ago."

"Not quite, but I was giving it serious consideration. No, really, my question concerns the inquest into the accidental death of Byron O'Hare. Do you remember that?"

The coroner's laugh track had suddenly been erased. I

152

could almost feel him hesitating. "Of course I do. I was new on the job. My first year. Very gung-ho. Old man Farley was the coroner. I was on the panel and doing some pathology work for the hospital."

There was no point in my trying to sneak up on him. I asked straight out if he could remember any points of controversy.

"Just one," he said. "And there was only one. It damn near cost me my certification."

He'd had thirty years to think it over and now, trying to reduce it to an anecdote, he had none of the youthful certainty of being in the right. Byron O'Hare was a famous man in his day, not front page famous like his brother the Governor, but a man of considerable reputation. So naturally the young assistant coroner had taken special pains to conduct a thorough autopsy.

"You must understand there was considerable pressure," he told me. "Alfred was *really* the Governor then, and he had all sorts of strings to pull, buttons to push. There was to be no suspicion of suicide, certainly nothing of foul play."

"And was he?" I asked. "Was Byron a suicide?"

I thought it was a legitimate question, since the impulse to self-destruct appeared to run in the family.

"In my opinion, no he was not. Not unless he succeeded in strangling himself. And as clever a fellow as Byron was, I don't think even he was capable of that."

It was, Nesmith informed me, a question of lividity marks and certain bruises on the shoulder and neck. In his enthusiasm he had theorized that the marks on Byron's body were consistent with those of human hands, and strong hands at that. Dr. Farley, who was senior to him, insisted that the marks were due to normal lividity and had been imprinted when Byron's body was retrieved from the water. At the inquest Farley's seniority had prevailed.

"To be perfectly honest," said Nesmith. "The only

reason I even testified was that like a fool I'd already filed my report. It was in the records and I had to stand by it. Believe me, I am not nearly so impetuous in my dotage."

Or so honest, I thought. I thanked Nesmith and hung up, feeling a little befuddled. I could imagine the fog rolling in off the sea, putting the seventh hole under a white mist. Somewhere in the mist was an eerie, birdlike squawking. A man deprived of air, held under water.

It was an interesting scenario. Pudge, a vigorous young man, holding his uncle under water until he'd drowned. But what was the motive? Certainly he wasn't *that* sore a loser. No one was driven to manslaughter over a game of golf, at least not on the amateur circuit. I had to treat the scenario in comic terms because it was too absurd to take seriously. Gentle Pudge, doting father, throttling his Uncle Byron? Impossible.

Unless. Pondering unless, I made myself a cheese omelette with a side of sausage, sliced open a pink Indian River grapefruit, and moved out to the sunporch. I tuned in Maine Public Radio, which was broadcasting something with a lot of sprightly violins in it, and settled into my rocker. I decided it was about time I started taking care of Connie. I was going to give up cigarettes and coffee and bourbon and thinking bad thoughts about people like Pudge O'Hare. I was going to give up bad language and fried food and sex with married policemen. I was going to dust off my Easter bonnet and go to church; in short, my hangover had been miraculously transformed into a halo and if it was still a little tight around the temples it would stretch with wearing.

With this new found piety, I mustered up the energy to sweep and mop the sunporch. I uncovered more layers of dirt than an archeologist. Botany was next on the agenda and I was giving Jesus Christ a transfusion when the telephone went off.

"Don't move," I told the avocado plant. "Don't drop even one leaf or it's over between us."

There was a heavy breather on the other end of the line. I could hear the air rattling through his nostrils and I was trying to think up a suitably wise remark when Truman Hawkins made himself known.

"Connie, uhmm I am, uh, at the Sutcliffe cottage." There was a rather long pause. I thought I heard a groan, or a muffled thump. When Truman continued his voice sounded strangely constricted. "I wanted to talk to Randy. But Tony Steel is here and he is . . ."

"What is he, Tru? What's going on down there?"

". . . is very upset. Tony is upset. He wants you to come down and explain a few things."

Now there was a definite thump and then the line went dead. My hands were slippery and cold and Richard's office number was refusing to come to the surface of my mind. I found it scrawled in the back of the address book. Richard wasn't there. I asked the desk sergeant to call him at home and relay my message.

I started out the door, turned, and ran back to the filing cabinet. I knew the pistol was loaded, checked it anyway to make sure, and slipped it into my purse. The tires on the rental Chevy must have been soft, because they squealed for most of a block, and Mrs. Hendriks, tending her roses, gave me a look that said *J'accuse.*

Chapter Nineteen

The tide was out at Sankaty Head. The dark under-
bellies of clouds were reflected on the mud flats where a
flock of gulls stalked the debris left behind by the retreating
sea. The wind was blowing out and on the steel blue hori-
zon of the north Atlantic white caps were forming. A white
sloop, hull down and driving with sails taut, rounded the
Head on a close tack for the harbor buoy.

Truman's beat-up Toyota was parked near the cottage,
front wheels deep into the beach grass. Pale pink beach
roses climbed a trellis over the gray shingles, weaving a
sparse covering over the high peaked roof of the converted
bath house. There were sparrows nesting around the central chimney; a couple of them fluttered up, complaining as
I approached. The walkway was formed of bleached stone
chips, and I kicked off my sandals and walked barefoot and
silent over the grass beside the walkway.

The pistol was in my right hand, pointed down and
away. As I came up to the door I debated returning the
damn thing to my purse. What if I had imagined the fear in

Truman's voice? Walking in unannounced with a loaded weapon was frowned on at the Head, as in most parts of the world.

I decided to risk being impolite. The paneled door was open a few inches. I didn't know what to make of that, except that I wouldn't have to knock. Listening at the door I heard two things: the thumping of my heart and a static, electronic buzzing.

The buzzing was coming from a pair of stereo speakers in the small, cozy living room. I don't know if Gerald was responsible for the furnishings. If so, he had a thing for black velvet pillows and prints of Impressionist painters: Renoir and his boat people, Cezanne and his fruits. I didn't bother calling out because there was no one stirring in that little room.

I located the stereo amplifier, which was built into the bookcases. A cassette was in the player. It had run all the way through and the volume was on maximum, hence the loud static background hiss in the speakers. There were pillows strewn about the planked pine floor, in a pattern that suggested neither a struggle nor a quest for comfort.

I didn't know what to make of it. I was hoping that Richard Stein would arrive before I had to check out the bedroom. He was taking his time, probably kissing the kids goodbye and giving Anne a squeeze. The son of a bitch. Didn't he know I had a phobia about black velvet pillows and cassette tapes run all the way through at full volume?

Not to mention antique beaded curtains that tingled as air moved through the cottage. I watched the beads move for a while, took a deep breath, and stepped through the curtain and into the bedroom.

It was a nice enough bedroom, with one queen-sized brass bed, covered in a patch quilt that someone had taken the trouble to smooth out while making the bed. Truman and Randy Joe Palowski were crouched on the floor near the bed. Their hands were tied up behind their backs with short lengths of clothesline. Their pale, blank faces were hugging the floor and the backs of their heads had been blown off.

The human brain doesn't look like much when it has leaked out of the skull cavity; it's hard to believe that a few cups of gray pudding contain a personality and the memories of a lifetime.

A black velvet pillow, blood spattered and leaking foam rubber from a pair of bullet holes, lay on the floor between the two bodies. Why waste your money on expensive silencers when you can crank up the stereo and muffle the shots in a pillow? Tony Steel had learned a lot during his six-month stay at Walpole; the pillow trick and how to tie nice neat square knots to bind the wrists, gangland style.

I wondered what Truman had uncovered that necessitated his execution. Or had he just been in the wrong place at the wrong time? No, I thought, give the man credit. He died because he knew more than *you* do. Truman looked so helpless in death, crouched forever with his hands lashed up behind him. I figured his hands had already been bound when he spoke to me. Not to mention a gun barrel jammed at his temple. Tru had done pretty good under the circumstances. I'd gotten the message and he'd gotten his head ventilated. I owed him.

Two cars came screeching in from opposite directions. The first contained Richard Stein, who was wearing a floral-design Hawaiian shirt hanging outside his khaki shorts except where the butt of his gun poked out of the waistband. George Krankow, the sheriff whose territory included Sankaty Head and environs, pulled himself out of the other car.

George was dressed in his summer uniform, complete with genuine pith helmet and aviator glasses. He had retired from the Navy as a Pentagon admiral and had run for sheriff because he needed something to keep him occupied. He was intelligent, if inclined to be more of a snob than the mostly snob set who had elected him. So far we'd managed to tolerate each other.

Seeing the pistol in my hand he drew his own. I looked at him and put the .32 back in my purse, very slowly. I sat down on the grass and practiced deep breathing while the two men went inside.

About five minutes later Richard came out and sat down beside me.

"You okay?"

I told him I was fine. Truman Hawkins wasn't feeling too good, thanks, but Connie Kale was fine. George Krankow came out, sighed heavily as he tugged at his creaking leather holster, and told us to wait a minute. He came back from his cruiser with a portable cassette recorder.

"Now, young lady, you'll tell us exactly what happened. First you'll tell us what happened before and after the phone call this reporter fellow made to you. Then it would be nice if you filled us in on what the hell you've been up to the last couple of weeks. Does that sound fair, Dick?"

Stein said it sounded fair indeed. Krankow set up the recorder on the grass, checked it out, and started the tape rolling. Richard lit me a cigarette, and fetched me a glass of cold water from the cottage. In the distance I could hear the ambulance siren coming down the shore road; it would make a nice touch on Krankow's tape, very atmospheric.

I supplied Krankow with a good long rambling account of how I had squandered my time and the Governor's money since Mandy's death. It takes longer to tell a story when you have to leave certain parts of it out. The idea being that the whole thing is still supposed to hang together somehow, so you must take care not to leave out essential cornerstones, lest the partial truths collapse of their own weight.

"Okay," said Krankow when he had an inch or so of my chatter on his machine. "Hawkins calls you, invites you to come down here to talk to Tony Steel. You say he sounds frightened. You leave a message for Dick and hurry down here, hoping to get yourself in the middle of a gun fight."

"I didn't say that."

"Mmm. I kind of think there is a lot you didn't say, young lady. You tell us both you and Hawkins had personal theories about some kind of extortion scheme. But you're not willing to be any more specific than that."

I told him that was as specific as I could get. Krankow was smiling, but there were little rubber hoses gleaming in his eyes. I decided to give him a more or less verbatim account of my interview with Arnold Maury.

"Now that's a little better, don't you think so, Dick?" Richard shrugged. He might have tried to wink at me, or maybe it was just dust in his eye. "We've read the file on the Maury brothers and extortion is certainly not unimaginable. What I want to know, supposing you and Hawkins are correct, is exactly what it is they were selling."

I shrugged and shook my head.

"Dirt on one of the O'Hare girls? You'd better level with us, Miss Kale. If Steel blew those two jokers in there away he might have the same thing in mind for you."

I ignored the last part of his statement. "Maybe Steel had some help, sheriff."

He asked me who I had in mind.

"No one in particular. Maybe a pro who works for the Maury brothers? This is just a theory."

"Just a theory," Krankow muttered. "Let's not muddle this up with theories. Right now for starters we have an

A.P.B. out on this slimeball Steel. We get him and we'll squeeze the rest of it out of him. Looks like a regular old 'falling out amongst thieves' to me."

"Or drug pushers," Richard said.

"Or blackmailers," I said.

"Yeah, well, take your pick," Krankow said, giving Stein a look that said stay on my side of the fence, chum. "My opinion, that doesn't matter right now. We have an aggregate of four homicides, we'll work that along before we worry about the blackmail angle."

I wondered if aggregate was a popular word in the Navy. Two more squad cars arrived, spilling out uniforms and one man in civilian dress only slightly less lurid than Richard's Hawaiian shirt: Tim Rosen in paint-spattered chinos and a tee-shirt emblazoned with the logo of the Atlanta Braves.

"Gee, the fag got it, huh? Too bad about Hawkins." He was excited and trying not to grin about it. "Close call for you, hey, Connie?"

I wasn't so sure, although I was not about to share my doubts with George Krankow or Richard Stein. The Governor was still my client and before I started chipping away at the family name I wanted to try and confirm the theory I'd been formulating about who was being blackmailed and why. I needed to follow up a lead that Truman Hawkins had inadvertently given me, without interference from the sheriff's department or the Rivermuth detective squad.

A van pulled up. A senior editor from the *Record* got out, along with a photographer. He recognized me and I saw him turn to the photographer and point my way.

"Look, guys," I said to the three cops. "If they run one of me on the front page I'm out of a job. Do I have permission to leave?"

Krankow grumbled, then snugged down his pith helmet and strode over to head off the press while Richard walked me to the rental Chevy. I told him if anyone had any more questions he could reach me at home. He didn't look like he believed me.

"Connie," he said, leaning in the window. I let him steal a quick kiss. "Now promise me you won't do anything dumb?"

I promised.

Chapter Twenty

The village of Pershing, Maine, overlooks the village of Pinesap, New Hampshire. The two villages are separated by a gorge that, at its lowest level, contains the shallow waters of the Pershing River. The bridge over the gorge is a popular spot for tourists, many of whom stop to toss a coin or two into the gorge. Once in a great while one of the tourists tosses himself or another over the rail, although this is a very rare occurrence and copper coins outnumber the bones in the river bed by a large margin.

My thoughts were on just such morbid events when I came down the steep incline into the village and stopped to ask directions at a one-pump gas station that might well have been outfitted from the pages of a 1928 Sears catalog. The attendant, an elderly gent with a cheek full of snuff and a few widely separated teeth, rattled off instructions in a manner that suggested long practice. But then Pershing was a place you passed through; if you wanted something there, chances are you were looking for Riverbend, the facility that has made Pershing quietly famous to a certain class of people. Riverbend is a kind of padded safe deposit box, where the wealthy deposit their insane.

Not that the word "insane" ever passes the lips of those who administer to the patients there. "Disturbed" is considered to be a *very* strong description of symptomatic behavior, and is reserved for those few poor devils who foam at the mouth and tear at the walls and befoul themselves with excrement.

I lied my way in by passing myself off as Kitty O'Hare, here to see my mother, Elisha.

"Oh dear," said Mrs. Beaudette, whose name was on a small white tag on her ample breast. "Elisha's regular physician isn't on today. He won't be back until Tuesday."

I had been counting on the fact that even a swank loony bin like Riverbend (which Mandy had called "Around-the-Bend") would be understaffed on Sundays. I had no idea how frequently Kitty visited her mother, if ever, and I was leery of being interviewed by Elisha's regular physician, who might have sniffed out my little impersonation.

"Oh, but I drove all the way out to this dreadful little village," I pouted. "And I *do* want to see Mummsie."

Mrs. Beaudette assured me that I could certainly see my mother. It was just that kin usually called ahead so that the attending specialist could be prepared for a briefing on the patient's status. My pouting and mini-tantrum had not fazed her in the least, and I sensed that Mrs. Beaudette had years of experience handling the wayward children of wacky inmates.

At her gentle suggestion I took a seat in the waiting area, which was a large, vegetation-strewn lobby painted in soothing pastels. I felt like curling up on the thick carpet and taking a nap under a potted palm, but there was a danger that I might wake up in a room with a view of the river and a door that only opened from the outside.

164

"Kitty? Hello, my name is Charles Pinchelli. I'm in charge of the East Wing on Sundays and holidays."

Pinchelli was in his mid twenties and wore a summer-weight poplin sports jacket. He was mildly pleasant to look at, except that his slightly poppish eyes reminded me of Truman. He sat down opposite me, holding a file folder.

"Are you a doctor?" The question was petulant, the way I imagined Kitty might be.

"I'm a psychologist. That is, I have a Master's in psych. But no, I'm not a medical doctor. Your mother's personal psychiatrist is here Tuesday through Saturday. However, if you'd like to visit your mother I'd be happy to brief you as best I can."

This was all rote. I could hear him reading it from the screen in his mind while he otherwise occupied himself by checking me out. I had purposefully worn a short skirt for just such a contingency and was perfectly willing to let the man distract himself visually if it would smooth the access to Elisha.

He opened the file. "Well, yes. As I'm sure you know your mother is a depressive type. In past years she has sometimes had a manic phase, which just means that she became very excited for a brief period of time, and subject to confusion and, er, delusions . . ." Pinchelli was scanning the file, trying to keep ahead of himself.

"I know about that," I said truthfully. "I was just a little girl when she came here to stay."

"Oh yes. Here it is. Your mother has been with us for seventeen years. Mmm. Originally as a detox patient."

"What's that?"

"Well, let's just say your mother had a drinking problem. She's long over that, of course. I see here she is on Elavil, which is a mood-altering drug, not addictive by the way. And of course a regular tranquilizer."

"What's a regular tranquilizer?"

"Uhmmm. Thorazine."

In other words, a drug strong enough to tranquilize a race horse. Reserved for the injection of thoroughbred crazies. It was reassuring in that I assumed Elisha would be too numb to cause an immediate scene if and when she realized that I was not her daughter Kitty. It was obvious that the attendant knew as little about the poor woman as I, and after a few minutes of forced chit-chat he got up and walked me to the East Wing.

We went through a recreation area that reminded me of a college dorm, except that it was much cleaner. A girl with short tufts of blonde hair was curled on a couch, listlessly watching Ingrid Bergman kiss an actor I did not recognize. I hoped it was the reflected luminescence of the television screen that made the girl's complexion look tinged with green. She couldn't have weighed more than seventy pounds.

My guide waited until we had passed through the double doors before commenting. "That's Carrie. She's much better. She's off intravenous and she's started eating. We've been seeing a lot of anorexics lately."

The way he said it implied that the disease was a fad with young women of the sort who could afford treatment at Riverbend. For all I know he might have been right, but I started to dislike him a little, and decided to call him Chuck.

"Kitty," he responded. "What's that short for?"

"It's not short for anything, Chuck. That's the name they gave me."

"How very droll," he said. His interest in my short skirt had worn off and he hurried me along. *Rich bitch,* oh I could almost see him thinking it, as if penned into a word balloon above his head.

I don't know what I expected to find at Riverbend. I assumed that straightjackets were long out of fashion and if there were bars on the windows they would probably be of

166

chic chromium steel and made to fit the decor. I supposed I
might find Elisha talking to the flower vase, or receiving
messages from outer space. More likely, comatose and
drugged out.

Instead I found a thin, bony woman wearing a dark
lavender sheath dress, a diamond bracelet, and several
rings. Her makeup was on straight and her hair had been
cut and set recently. I would not have described her eyes as
vivacious, neither were they obviously drugged. She was in
a lounge on the screened-in porch adjacent to her suite and
when Chuck Pinchelli announced me an attendant had just
finished replenishing a tall glass of iced tea.

Elisha said nothing until Pinchelli and the attendant
had withdrawn. I stood in the middle of the porch, trying to
remember the lines I had rehearsed.

"Your dress is too short," said Elisha. "You have dimpled knees. Also you are not Kitty."

The fact that I was not her daughter didn't seem to
bother her. There was a buzzer on the side of a table within
reach of her lounge. She looked at the buzzer and then
back to me.

"No," I said. "I made that up. I'm not Kitty. My name
is Connie Kale. I'm, ah, a friend of Mandy's."

"Haven't you heard?" said Elisha. Her voice was flat,
lacking intonation. "Mandy is dead. If you're a friend of
hers I assume you would know that."

My knees, dimples and all, were weak. I pulled over a
chair and sat down. "Yes, I know about Mandy, Mrs.
O'Hare. That's sort of why I'm here."

"But why did you say you were Kitty?"

"So I could get in to see you. I thought it would be
easier that way."

Elisha nodded. Her eyes wandered from me to the
open balcony. The porch was a few feet above a rolling
lawn. I could see a line of spruce trees and the edge of the
meadow where the gorge began. We sat like that for a very

long minute as I waited for Elisha to speak. She didn't appear to be interested in continuing the conversation.

"I'm glad you're not Kitty," she said finally, without emotion. "Kitty has never come here. It would make me nervous if you were really Kitty."

An opening. I decided to jump in. "Did Mandy make you nervous?" I asked. "When she came to see you recently?"

"No." Elisha thought about it for a while, sipping her tea and not looking at me. "Mandy made me laugh."

Elisha made it sound as if laughter were a physical reaction to a specific stimulus, like hitting your knee to make your leg jerk.

"He came to tell me she was dead," said Elisha without any prompting. "They thought I would be upset. Of course I was not upset. We're all dead already. Alfie is dead and Mandy is dead and Kitty is dead and 'Lisha is dead. Everybody."

I found it difficult to formulate a response. I was beginning to understand what Elisha was doing at Riverbend. She had deadened herself to emotion to the degree that all contact with life was extinguished.

"Who came to tell you? Was it Pudge?"

Elisha shrugged indifferently. "He's dead, too. He made those funny crying noises and he wanted me to pray with him. Isn't that absurd?" She took her glass of iced tea and emptied it on the floor, for no reason that I could fathom.

From the porch I could see a woman in a pale pink gown walking through the meadow toward the river. Pinchelli was walking behind her, hands in his pockets as if out for a stroll. When the woman in the gown got within range of the gorge he headed her off, steering her back toward the East Wing. When the woman walked she bounced, as if on hidden springs, and her thin arms fluttered up like tendrils of seaweed in a swelling tidal pool. As if Riverbend were underwater and we were drowning, all of us.

"Elisha," I said, "Do you remember why Mandy came to visit you?"

She shifted on her lounge and stared down at the melting ice cubes on the porch floor. "Look what you did. I have to pay for those. That costs money and ice doesn't grow on trees."

Riverbend was starting to infect me, because I knew what she meant. Outside, the woman in the long pale gown was bouncing toward the gorge again, and Chuck was heading her off. He still had his hands in his pockets and he reminded me of a stern Groucho Marx. Not that there was anything amusing about the game he was playing with the bouncer.

"I give myself a present for my birthday," Elisha was saying. She unclipped her diamond bracelet and dropped it into the glass she'd emptied of ice. "I attempt suicide. That's my present to myself. This year I used the sash from one of my robes. The knot slipped. I knew it would."

"I don't understand," I said truthfully. Somehow the ice melting on the porch was numbing my brain, blunting the part of me that should have been feeling pity for Elisha. "If you're already dead, why bother to kill yourself?"

She put the glass containing the bracelet down on the table beside her. "Exactly. I don't *really* try to kill myself. It is just an attempt. I do it every year a different way. It's just something to do. There's not a lot to do here, you know."

I disagreed. There was loads to do, what with watching television and bouncing into the gorge and attempting suicide. It could be a fun place if you were already dead. I was picking up on a trend, because after ten minutes with Elisha I found that Truman's death no longer seemed very real. And in a way it was his fault that I was there, since he had found out about Mandy's visit. I decided I had better leave soon, before I found myself in a long gown, walking with Groucho Marx.

"Do you remember Byron, Elisha?"

She had picked up the glass from the table and was sloshing her bracelet around. "Byron?" she said, with something like animation. "He's the one who started it all, you know. He was the first one to find out about dying."

There was no fighting it. Death was her one area of interest. "What happened when he drowned in that pond, Elisha, do you know?"

She sighed. It was obvious that I wasn't very bright, in her opinion. "What does it matter? Byron told me we were all born a moment from being dead and that we just had to wait a certain number of years before it happened."

"When did Byron tell you that, Elisha?"

"Oh, when he was fucking me."

I woke up. I was no longer numb. I remembered why I was there. "Byron made love to you, Elisha?"

She shrugged, staring at the glass as she rattled the bracelet. "Byron brought me vodka. That was when they wouldn't let me drink."

"You mean he got you drunk and then took you to bed?"

"Fucking doesn't hurt much," she said. "I didn't care. I just wanted to drink the vodka. All of it. All of the vodka in the world."

It happened so fast that I couldn't stop her. Elisha tipped up the glass and swallowed the bracelet. I shouted for the attendant, who must have been waiting just outside the door, because she was beside me by the time I had Elisha bent over, pounding her back.

"No, not like that. Here, you hold her mouth open. Watch out for the teeth."

It was like prying open a steel trap. The nurse amazed me. She simply reached back into Elisha's mouth and came back out with the bracelet hooked around her fingers.

Elisha stopped choking immediately. The nurse shook her head and patted Elisha's cheek.

"Wasn't that funny?" said Elisha in her dead voice. "And it's not even my birthday. Wasn't that funny?"

I got the hell out of there, before I started thinking it was funny, too.

Dusk was deep and blue at Sankaty Head, like an evening in a painting by Maxfield Parrish. I half expected to see Grecian nymphs frolicking in the twilight, as serene as only the children of gods can be. But there were no children of gods in Sankaty Head. There never had been.

The drive back from the asylum had taken an hour or so. I had taken it slow, using the time to drive away the trembles and bang out the dents the visit with Elisha had put in my psyche. I went over how to break my latest blackmail theory to the Governor. He was not going to be happy, no matter how discreetly I laid it out for him.

It must have been the maid's night off, because Dr. Sutcliffe answered the bell himself.

"Oh, hello, Connie. You're rather late with your report, dear. The police were here this afternoon. That Jewish fellow and the sheriff who dresses up like Jungle Jim."

Good old Sutcliffe. I knew I could depend on him to be in character, no matter what transpired. He told me that Pudge had been driven up to Falmouth Foreside, to address the Young Republicans. The Governor was gone and he was not expected back that evening.

"Is he with Pudge? I have to see him, Doc, it's very important."

"Oh, I'm sure *everything* you do is important, dear. It must have been gruesome for you, finding those two bodies at the bathhouse. Gerald ought not to rent to trash like that."

"The Governor?"

171

"He left right after the police were here. I don't think he's very pleased with your work, dear."

I told him I wasn't too pleased with it myself. I put on an expression of fierce determination. I wanted Sutcliffe to think that I was going to find out where the Governor was if I had to shove pins under his fingernails. He was so terrified that he chuckled and shook his head.

"He didn't tell me where he was going, Connie. I'm not his appointments secretary, you know."

I didn't know what he was in relation to the O'Hares. Brother-in-law, next-door abortionist, drug dispenser, take your pick.

"Look, I have to see the Governor and I have to see him tonight. I know you think I'm being melodramatic, but it could be a question of life and death. Pudge's life."

Sutcliffe mumbled and grumbled. Finally he admitted that while Alfred had not said where he was going, his mood indicated that he wanted solitude, and Sutcliffe guessed that the old man was heading for serenity.

"What? Heading for where?"

"'Serenity.' Byron's retreat. The building was never finished, but Himself goes there at certain times. He was very upset to hear about Mr. Steel. So if you really must disturb him, you can try 'Serenity.'"

He was kind enough to draw me a map.

Chapter Twenty-one

I was on the road, several different ones, for hours.
The car radio kept me company. It sang me songs like Fats
Waller's "Savin' My Love For You" and Ella giving me
"Miss Otis Regrets." When that signal faded I fiddled
around and got a country station. Maine has more cowboys
per square mile than any state east of Montana, if country
stations and gun-rack pickups are any indication. That's
okay by me. Willie Nelson can sing "Honeysuckle Rose"
until the thorns fall off. I sang along, my head sparking
with caffeine and adrenalin. I got the coffee at an all-night
diner; the adrenalin was my very own.

At the news break a local announcer told me that
thunder showers were expected inland and that the latest
indications showed Pudge O'Hare, son of the former governor, in the lead for the first time in polls of the Republican
primary.

"Maybe for the last time," I told the announcer. He
shut me up with a dose of Freddy Fender.

It was not quite midnight when I got to the unmarked
logging road on Dr. Sutcliffe's hand-drawn guide to "Se-

renity." According to my speedometer I was a quarter of a mile beyond the juncture of routes 3 and 3A. If I was in the right place there should be a chain-link fence, a gate post, and a sign proclaiming PRIVATE ACCESS, ROAD CLOSED.

I left the Chevy running with the radio on and got out with a flashlight to see what I could see. The sign jumped out into the pool of light. There was a chain wrapped around the gate post. On closer inspection it was not padlocked, merely looped. I held the flash in my teeth and unknotted the chain. My hands were trembling. It must have been the coffee.

After I'd pushed open the gate I ran the light around and found fresh tire tracks on the hard packed dirt road.

"He come this way, Kemo Sabe, driving many horses," I said aloud. I got back in the Chevy, put the transmission in low, and started the two-mile climb to the peak.

Byron O'Hare hadn't been a man who did things in half measures. When he built a golf course it was of championship quality, and when he decided to build himself a weekend retreat he bought a mountaintop and had a road carved up to it. Sutcliffe had told me there were no power lines, no telephone, and that electricity was provided by a small generating plant fueled by diesel engines.

Fat drops of rain spattered the dirt in front of the headlights and quickly blurred the windshield. Whoever was in charge of the special effects was right on cue. A rainy night, a dark mountain, a ruined castle. All it needed was a mad scientist, a one-eyed hunchback, and a private investigator with a bad case of nerves.

The road was a switchback, cut into the mountainside at an incline so steep that I felt as if I had to cling to the wheel to keep from falling backwards. The engine bucked and wheezed as I concentrated on the narrow strip under the headlamps, ignoring the black emptiness yawning from the lip of the rutted road.

The drops of rain got smaller and quicker as they multiplied. I put the wipers on high and that helped, although I was more concerned with a washout than with being able to see. Part of the problem was that my mind was racing while the car chugged upward at a speed that barely jerked the needle on the speedometer.

I came around one final switchback and the roadbed leveled off. There were stunted pines on one side, a vertical ledge on the other, and a Mercedes sedan directly in front of me. I know because I almost crunched the bumper. When I shut the engine off I could hear the rain drumming the car top. My umbrella was in the Duster, which was in the junkyard. I stood outside the car and tried to get my bearings. The rain was coming straight down in torrents. Still, the rain wasn't cold; after the initial shock, it wasn't quite as miserable as I thought it might be.

The beam of the flashlight was stunted by the downpour. Fortunately the Governor had parked the Mercedes directly opposite a set of steps, which had been made up of huge granite slabs, stacked and mortised together. The storm had turned the steps into a cascade of miniature waterfalls. I sloshed upward, trying to shield my eyes with one hand while aiming the flash with the other.

At the top of the steps I came out of the lee of the ledge. Wind drove the rain into me, chilling and sharp. Overhead an explosion of steel beams protruded from the blasted granite, vaulting upward to hold big rectangles of raw concrete. The rectangles were the interconnected parts of "Serenity." Byron O'Hare must have been an ironic man to choose such a name for his startling piece of unfinished architecture. The place was about as serene as a Stravinsky symphony. I could see lights coming from the gunslit windows on the lowest level, however, and I was more than willing to treat it as a sanctuary.

I ducked under a wing of the superstructure and caught my breath. There were no gutters and the water raced along the overhead beams. I would have been surprised to find a doorbell; it was the sort of place you signaled by rocket from another mountaintop. The door was the type used in a commercial warehouse, jacketed in gray steel. I beat my fist against it and was pleased by the booming noise. I was willing to wake the dead to get out of the wind and rain.

It took a while. I was starting to get into the rhythm and resonance when the bolt was drawn and the door cracked open.

"Governor? It's me, Connie Kale."

He admitted that he had not recognized me. The door shut long enough for him to release the chain and then I was inside. I had to resist the impulse to shake myself off like a dog as Alfred O'Hare stared at me, waiting for an explanation.

I had been expecting to confront an angry man. Instead I found him exhausted, and for the first time in my experience, elderly. He was wearing a thick, brushed velour robe over slacks and slippers and he admitted that I had awakened him.

"You gave me quite a shock, young lady. This isn't a place where one expects to have someone drop by in the middle of the night. Come along, I'll find you something dry to put on."

We were standing in a sort of scooped-out stairwell. Bolt heads from the forms still protruded from the raw concrete walls, bleeding rusty stains. A welded steel staircase curved up to a higher level, with treads of unpolished slate that vibrated dully under our feet. I used the handrail; Alfred O'Hare went up unaided, his back and shoulders as straight as a nun's steel ruler. As he glanced sideways at me I saw concern, possibly a glint of fear. I thought: he already knows something of the news I bring.

The upper level was wide open, an immense slab of reinforced concrete with a few rugs thrown down haphazardly. A round, black-chuted fireplace stood in the middle of the room. There was a fire burning in it, and a long curved couch stood just outside the flickering circle of firelight. A wooden-spoked captain's chair had been placed near to the fire, with a rolling bar at arm's reach. I assumed the Governor had been napping on the couch, under the sheepskin cover that was turned back.

"This was going to be partitioned into smaller rooms," he told me. "But I've left is as it is. I like the space. When I fall asleep next to the fire I almost imagine I'm outside, sleeping under the stars."

Only a few of the wall bracket lights were on and the outside walls, which jutted out, seemed to fade into the distance, skewing perspective. The place reminded me of an abandoned airport lounge somewhere in the Twilight Zone, or the ruined command bridge of a ferro-concrete battleship. I realized how foolish it was of us children to think that Byron had haunted the pond at the seventh green. He had been here all along, in the raw cold bones of his unfinished masterpiece.

"Here you are," said the old gentleman wearily. "I think this will be warm enough. And the towel. I'll sit right here in my chair and look the other way."

He handed me a spare robe and a towel and I retreated into the darkness. The Governor sat with his back to me, in silhouette against the firelight as I stripped off my drenched clothes, toweled myself dry, and slipped into the thick, quilted robe. The robe smelled like Alfred O'Hare; the mingled odor, partly imagined, of old money and expensive Scotch, with the faint scent of the tonic he used to keep his thinning white hair scooped straight back on his old man's skull.

He nodded to me when I sat down on the couch, tucking my legs up under me. I took the Scotch on ice he handed me. It was not my usual drink, but it would do. I sipped it as the Governor poked at the fire with a shortened length of reinforcing rod.

"Let me guess," he said. "They picked up that guinea stripper, they arrested him, and now he's out on bail again." When he looked at me his face turned into a shadow and I could no longer see his eyes. "With what speed they tip out the scales of justice, hey girl?"

I told him that as far as I knew Tony Steel was still at large. I was confident that he would be picked up soon enough. It was not about Steel that I had come, not directly. The old man was drinking his booze straight and he deliberately drained his glass and poured another. He leaned down and put the new glass on the floor beside him and then sat back up, his hands folded in his lap.

"You'd better tell me what you know, girl. You wouldn't have driven all this way on this hellish night if you didn't have something to break my heart with."

I'd put it together a dozen different ways over the past few hours. There was no good way to begin and I had not yet come to any conclusions as to how it should end. So I simply told him. I did my best not to let the words tumble out, and to try and put them in a reasonable order.

When I was done the Governor picked up the drink from the floor. He stared at it, leaving it undrunk. Maybe he liked the way the firelight flickered through the bottom of the glass.

"Now let me get this straight," he said after a long pause. "I've been through a lot in the last few days and my brain is getting creaky."

He dipped his finger in the glass of Scotch and then rubbed the finger around his gums. It was an intimate gesture, like watching a man at the toilet, and it made me feel uneasy and at the same time strangely close to him.

"You theorize that Mandy had access to information that was vitally damaging to her father, possibly information the police would have been keenly interested in. That's the first part. The second part you're not sure of. Either Mandy let this information slip to Jon Maxfield or, out of sheer perversity and mischief, she sold it to him. He in turn contacted Pudge, demanding payment to keep this information out of the public—not to say police—eye. Then on the night the payment is made the blackmailer, Maxfield, goes to the motel room where Mandy and his colleague are . . . 'shacked up'? Is that still the way they say it? Something of a violent nature occurs. If we are generous we assume that Mandy changed her mind about surrendering this information and Maxfield stabbed her. Or possibly he was jealous of her relationship with the other stripper and *that* is why he stabbed her . . ."

He took his time drinking the Scotch and then returned the empty glass to the floor before continuing. "But why he stabbed Mandy is not really important. The fact is that he did and then he went out into the alley behind the motel. Waiting in the alley was the man he was blackmailing. My son Pudge. Here there is a divergence of theory. Either Maxfield had arranged to meet Pudge there for the payoff, or Pudge followed him to the motel, saw him stab Mandy, and then waited outside for him. That doesn't really matter, either. What matters is that you think Pudge killed Maxfield."

The old man turned the chair so that he was facing me. The tone of his recitation suggested that very little of what I had told him came as a surprise.

"Tell me, dear. Do you classify Maximum Jon Maxfield as a human being? Do you think that his being extinguished lessened the quality of life?"

I thought: it surely lessened the quality of *his* life. I did not say it. I had had my say, now the Governor was having his.

"He was left out there in the muck like the garbage he was, girl. Like the garbage he was. You'll pardon an old man's prejudices, but I consider his disposal a service to the community. Blackmail is just an exotic form of suicide. Maybe Pudge held the knife, but that two-legged scum threw himself on it, the way I see it."

He got up from the chair and tightened the sash of his robe. He picked up the length of reinforcing rod and poked at the embers. A shower of sparks spilled out of the grate and down to the concrete floor. He could not help posing a little by the light of that fire, aware of his own profile, which was still handsome, especially in the soft light. If the situation had been different I think he might have tried seducing me, just to see if he still had the power in him.

He carried a bottle over to me and replenished my drink. "It's good for the gums, you know. Kills infection. I still have all of my teeth, thanks to those miserable Scots and their marvelous whiskey."

I thanked him for the drink, and for the advice, and then we both waited. The old man paced around the circular fireplace, one hand in the pocket of the robe, the other holding his drink. I sat quietly on the sofa with my legs tucked up, pacing on the inside.

"The theory is interesting, as far as it goes," he said at last. "One thing bothers me. This 'secret' information my son was supposedly being blackmailed for. What was it? Do you know?"

My legs were starting to tingle. I straightened them out, moving my bare feet to get the blood circulating. "What I have," I said, "is just another theory. For a while I thought it had something to do with drugs. Cocaine. Maxfield was known to be dealing. He was undoubtedly selling the stuff to Mandy. Also he works for a man who is suspected of running a major league drug operation out of Portland. But it kept coming back to this: Mandy is buying cocaine. So what? Who cares?"

"So what?"

"Sure. So what if Maxfield can prove that Mandy uses coke, or buys it, or even sells it? He might be able to squeeze a little juice with that information, just to keep the law out of her hair. But even if she was busted for use or for dealing, I couldn't see it substantially hurting Pudge's campaign. Not nowadays. The public is pretty sophisticated about drugs, and also about children. No one, not even here in good old 'So Goes the Nation' Maine, is really going to blame a father for what his adult daughter is doing with drugs. The popular consensus, which is what we're talking about here, the popular consensus is that it is *not* the parents' fault. For all we know Pudge might even have got some sympathy votes if Mandy was arrested on drug charges. Just like he's getting sympathy votes because she was murdered."

I stopped. I thought maybe I was going too far in discussing the effects of Mandy's death so coolly. After all, the man was her grandfather. She was his blood. He had to feel something, even if he had written her off years ago. But he had returned to the chair by the fire and situated himself in such a way that I could not see his face. He flapped his hand, urging me to continue, or maybe to finish.

"Whatever, the drug stuff was not information worth dying—or killing for. It had to be something devastating, to make a man like Jon Maxfield risk going back to prison. It had to be worth big money. And that's when I started feeding Byron into the equation."

The Governor seemed to relax in his chair. I think he had been waiting for me to say the name.

"You managed to force the inquest to reach the verdict you wanted. You were the governor then, and you had the kind of influence that can sway a coroner's report. Especially when there was no motive. Pudge was a nice young man. No history of violence. Why ever should he have wanted to murder his uncle Byron? Why should he knock him backward into the pond and hold his head underwater?"

I was a little surprised to find that I was on my feet, both hands before me with fingers extended. I dropped my hands, hiding them in the voluminous folds of the borrowed robe.

"You tell me," said Alfred O'Hare. "Why should he?"

"I couldn't figure it out," I said. "Until this afternoon. When I dropped in to visit Elisha. And she told me that Byron had filled her up with vodka and taken her to bed. She was a real looker in her time, wasn't she, Governor? She must have been a real temptation to a middle-aged bachelor like Byron. Right there in that big house, alone with her problems, too weak to bother resisting him?" .

I moved so that I could see his face clearly. The only thing discernible there was the passing of time and an ancient weariness.

"Elisha was a basket case," he said. "She couldn't help herself. I think she quite literally sold her body for a bottle of vodka. Isn't that sad? A rich roman in a millionaire's mansion, selling herself for a bottle of vodka?"

It was more than sad. It was enough to make a man want to kill. To make him run from the bedroom where his drunken wife slurred the truth to him. To make him run down that narrow path to the golf course where he knew that Byron, feeling young and virile and conquering, was treating himself to a congratulatory game of golf. A postcoital stab at par.

"I don't think it was premeditated murder," I said. "I think he was so angry he didn't know what he was doing. I think he leaped on Byron and they rolled and fought by the water's edge. And he was strong enough and young enough to hold Byron under. It wouldn't take long, not if both men were angry and fighting and out of breath. Maybe less than a minute."

The old man was poking at the fire again. He wasn't doing much good. The embers were burning down. The fire needed more fuel and the jabbing steel bar was dividing

182

flame against flame, smothering the heat under a pile of cooling ashes.

"That was so many years ago," he said. "So much has happened since then. I think what happened to Byron was an accident, in the best sense of the word. Sometimes our hearts hurt too much and there is an accident."

"Could be. But it's the kind of 'accident' a blackmailer can get a lot of mileage out of. A lot of money."

He left the poker in the dying fire and stood up.

"And what about what happened today, to your friend the reporter? How do you fit that into your theory, girl? Don't try tying my son to *that*. He was a hundred miles away when it happened."

I agreed. It was not Pudge's style at all. Not the hands tied behind the back, the bullets calmly pumped into the base of the skull. It was a professional job, and that meant outside talent. No, Pudge hadn't been at the cottage, but his newest blackmailer was. That was why Randy had camped himself so near to the Head. All the better to continue the scheme that Jon Maxfield had started. Maximum Jon had successfully extracted a large sum from Pudge, who was now doubly vulnerable for having been at the scene of his daughter's death, and Randy had been executed for that money and for what it represented.

Access.

"Don't you see it?" I said. I could feel the Scotch in my head, the heat of it in my throat. "The big guns are in now. Randy and Tony and Maxie are small-timers. But Arnold Maury and his organization are biggies. They'll break Pudge. They'll hold off for a while, hoping he gets elected, and then they'll bleed him dry. I don't know how much Pudge has paid out so far, but whatever it is it will be nothing compared to what comes later."

At that moment Alfred O'Hare looked much older than his seventy-odd years. He was as old as the landscape, as old as the mountain, and his eyes were deep holes drilled into the basalt. I got the feeling that he'd already heard everything I had to say to him, that a voice had been whispering to him since the morning when he went down to identify his granddaughter's body.

He came up close to me. I could smell the booze on his breath, and the weariness. "You've told me what you came to tell me, Miss Kale. You have made your report, exactly as I hired you to do, to me and to me alone. Now I have a question. What are you going to do about it?"

This was the hard part. This is what had been frazzling me all the way back from Riverbend and all the way up to Byron's mountain. I had been turning it around and inside out, looking for the seams, looking for a way out. And I had finally decided that I was going to do what I most hated doing in the world: let a man make the decision for me.

I told him. He stepped back, looking me up and down. He wasn't admiring my body, he was trying to feel his way inside me and see if I meant what I said.

"You surprise me, girl. You don't expect me to turn my own son in, do you?"

I shook my head. My hair was still damp and strands of it stuck to my cheeks. "No. But you do have to protect him somehow. Maury and his boys will eat him alive. It will be worse if he actually gets himself elected. I'm leaving it up to you, Alfred," I said, using his name for the first time. "I think Pudge killed Maxfield because he saw him stab Mandy. I know he loved her. He came out to my house, drunk as a skunk and weeping, to tell me so. . . ."

"Weak," muttered the old man. "*Weak.*"

". . . and it's unlikely that the County Prosecutor could put together a case against him for drowning Byron, not after thirty years. But we'll have to convince him to withdraw from the race and we'll have to go to the Special Drug Task Force and let them know what the Maury brothers are up to. They're in a position to do something about it."

184

The Governor was nodding. He had both hands in the pockets of his robe and despite the robust stature of his body he looked frail, as if he were shrinking into himself.

"Come with me," he said softly. "There's something you should see, before we break it to Pudge. Something Byron left here. A legacy."

I followed him outside the circle of light. Rain was still spitting against the gunslit windows. It sounded as if the storm was abating. In five or six hours the sun would be breaking in through those slits, projecting itself across the cold acre of concrete like the prism beam of a spectroscope.

We went down a spiral staircase in a concrete tube that reminded me of a lighthouse tower. The rough walls were sweating moisture and at the bottom there was a puddle where the rain had forced its way inside. Under the stairs was a steel-jacketed door fitted with a heavy industrial lock. The old man fished a key from the floppy pockets of his robe, braced his shoulder against the door, and opened it.

He motioned me inside while he fumbled for the light. There was another of the peculiar gunslit-shaped windows high overhead. I could see it as a slightly darker oblong before the light came on.

"At your feet, girl," said the Governor. "What do you think of that?"

When I had blinked away the spots before my eyes I looked down and saw a body. The body was trussed up with white clothesline, neatly knotted. Then the body shifted and I realized, with a second shock, that it was alive. The mouth was firmly gagged with a torn undershirt, but I recognized the dark Sicilian eyes. It was Mandy's slow dancer, her man of steel.

It didn't take much in the way of intuition to know that Alfred O'Hare would be holding a gun when I turned around. It was a police .38 with a snub barrel. Just the thing for muzzling in black velvet pillows.

"Lie down," he said.

His expression was featureless. I was confused and my head was pounding and I did not want to lie down on the damp concrete floor.

He shot me. That is the pistol flared and the hem of my robe jumped where it had been pierced by a bullet. In that hollow room the detonation and ricochet roared and my ears felt as if they had been slapped by an iron fist.

I dropped to the floor. He had a length of clothesline ready, coiled and stored in the same pocket where he'd kept the pistol. I lay next to the dancer, my wrists bound up behind me and connected by a short loop to my ankles. The belt from the robe was between my teeth and the next explosion I heard was the steel door slamming shut.

Chapter Twenty-two

In the beginning I was glad of the darkness. I imagined that Tony Steel would be looking at me with accusing eyes. My thoughts lacked coherence and in my scattered way I must have thought his face would be a mirror of my own. The floor under me was hard and rough, but the only real pain was the numbness spreading from my wrists. I tried shifting into a better position, anything to take the strain off the rope. I tucked my knees up under my chin, lying sideways, and that helped a little.

After a while the darkness began to have a depth and a shape all its own. I used it to project my own shapes and thoughts and gradually was able to bring myself under control. I needed to be under control so I could find the answer to a question. The wrong answer had landed me there in the dark, bound and trussed and ready for an execution; now I wanted the right answer. Not that the right answer would untie my wrists or disarm the Governor. I just wanted to *know*.

I kept adding it up and the sum kept coming out the same and that was completely crazy because the figure that negated the entire equation was lying next to me. I had been thinking that Byron dead equals Pudge equals blackmail equals Mandy dead at the Sea Breeze Motel. Now I was being forced to scrub that and replace part or all of it with the Governor and no matter how I tried to make it fit none of it made sense.

Unless the Governor was working for Pudge. Unless the son was running the father, which flew in the face of all that I had observed. I tried to remember the certainty I'd felt when I came up to that door in the rain. I had suspected then that the Governor knew most or all of what I was about to tell him. What I had not suspected was that he had been drawn into taking an active part.

Okay. With a little shaping and pushing I could almost make it hold together: the devoted daddy doing his best to save his boy's good name. But what about the dancer? Why was he alive in the dark beside me? Why wasn't he back there on the floor of the converted bathhouse with his brains blown out, like Truman Hawkins and Mrs. Palowski's son, Randy Joe, saint name Timothy?

To distract myself from the dual pain of having my wrists tied and being wrong, I started watching the slightly darker rectangle of the gunslit window. Maybe when dawn broke I would wake up and find myself on the couch upstairs, befuddled by a strange nightmare inspired by too much of the Governor's Scotch whiskey. That shows you the sort of straws I was clutching at. The window actually was starting to lighten when I heard the key in the lock.

It was just light enough to try making eye contact with Tony Steel. A mistake. The fear I saw there was immediately injected into me. I'd thought that the drive up to the mountaintop had pretty much squeezed my adrenal cortex dry, but there were enough dregs left to shorten my breath and start my heart doing a steel drum reggae against my rib cage.

The overhead light came on. I was ready for that and

was squinting my eyes. The Governor still had the pistol in one hand. In the other he had a glass containing several fingers of what looked like straight Scotch. He was dressed, wearing chinos and Pendleton and a new pair of Sperry Topsiders. Except for the .38 he might have stepped right out of an L.L. Bean mail-order catalogue. Your typical upper-crusty, backwoodsy society killer.

He tucked the pistol in his waistband, took hold of my shoulders, and propped me up against one wall. The flap of the robe was matted under me and he readjusted that, covering my nakedness. He then took the pistol out and sat down on his haunches, his back against the opposite wall. The dancer lay between us, his eyes squeezed shut. I assumed he was trying to make himself invisible. Even if he had been able to make his body incorporeal, the sharp odor of sweat and urine would have given him away.

"I've been thinking," said the Governor. He picked up the glass and looked it over. "Also I have been drinking."

He seemed to be waiting for a response. I tried nodding and hoped to communicate a willingness to engage in endless dialogue, if only he would consent to remove the gag from my mouth.

"You know what fascinates me?" he said. "This whole myth we have about sleep. All that nonsense about the eight-hour cycle and the dangers of sleep deprivation. Well, take it from me, young lady. Sleep is a waste of time. I mean that quite literally. For the last thirty years I have never slept more than four hours out of twenty-four, and since Mandy died I've had none at all. Just a few cat naps, to rejuvenate my body."

That might explain the intense dilation of his pupils. Alfred O'Hare looked capable of inhaling me through his eyes. And not only me, but Tony Steel and the room and the mountaintop. He was wearing the eyes of a madman and that frightened me almost as much as the snub nosed .38.

"And dreams," he said, with his new intensity. "I swear to you that I have not had a dream in thirty years. Not since Byron and I had our fight and I won."

He waited. I tried nodding again, *isn't that nice, guv, that you won, now will you please untie me?* I had the eerie sensation that he was looking right through me, possibly right through the poured concrete wall.

"Because I did win, you know. You got most of it right, girl. That was the part you got wrong. Pudge is a good boy. He never had it in him to drown Byron. Just like he never really had it in him to make love to Elisha, not like she needed it. He got the weakness from his mother's side of the family, and I've had to stand in for him for most of his life. Not that I'm complaining, mind you. Just stating a fact.

"That was why I hired you, girl. To get the facts to me without worrying the boy about things that had to be done. You were my private snitch and I think you did an excellent job. You're very bright and intuitive. If I was going to have Pudge remarry I would consider you for the job, dear."

He waited again, smiling mildly. I'd given up on nodding so I shrugged my shoulders and tried to look bright and bridelike. Marry Pudge? Sure, why not? But it was hard to look like an eligible bride-to-be when I was tied up and wrapped in an old man's bathrobe. Also my hair was a mess.

For the first time he seemed to be aware of the dancer. He reached out and prodded him with his yet-to-be-scuffed Topsider and the man of steel jerked. I felt bad for him. He looked even worse than I did and his hands were as swollen as the corpse of his pal Maxie. I could see where he'd tried to work himself free and the rope had cut into him and already scabbed over.

"I suppose you're wondering what I'm doing with this," he said, meaning Tony Steel. "Taking him alive was an impulse thing, but I've learned to trust my impulses. I'll be the first to admit my temper has gotten me into trouble. I have this problem with perspective, dear. I've never told anyone this, but when I am truly angry I feel a power in me. I feel like a vengeful god, looking down from a storm cloud. I think that's what happened to me the night Mandy died. Killing her there was a mistake. I should have waited and arranged an accident."

He decided to tell me all about it. How he had been approached by Maxfield, who had taken some compromising Polaroids of Mandy. Snapshots that in any year but an election year would not have had any particular value.

"I never even looked at them," said the Governor. "I just gave Maxfield his ten thousand and tore the pictures to shreds. I think he was surprised that I didn't want to take a peek. He thought I was a dirty old man, dying to peep on my own granddaughter."

That was when the temper started to bother him. Maxfield had contacted him by telephone and arranged to meet in the parking lot of the Play Pen Lounge. Okay, fine, Maxfield would get his first payment and the Governor would find out exactly who and what he was and then have him destroyed by conventional methods. Even after all those years Alfred O'Hare still had friends in the state police and in the judiciary who would help him destroy a cretin like Jon Maxfield.

But then Maxfield had gloated. Maximum Jon had just squeezed ten grand from an old man, a rich old man, and he was determined to get maximum pleasure out of it. So he told grampa exactly what was in the snapshots he had so hastily destroyed.

"He was a sick thing," said the Governor. "He was not even slightly human. It made my skin crawl to be there with him. I was starting to have this impulse about running him over, squashing him like the bug he was, when Mandy came up out of that bar."

It was the kind of coincidence that eventually kills four people, six if you counted the dancer and me as good as dead. Failing to find her new stud Maxie, she had picked up his friend Tony as a substitute. Maxie, you see, was being a busy little bee blackmailing her grandfather, but Mandy didn't know that. Nor did she know that cunning and too-clever Maxie had culled enough information out of her to know who really wore the pants in her family.

Mandy's fatal mistake was walking out into the night with her arm around another male stripper. And if there had been any doubt, Maxie dispelled it by telling the Governor exactly who Tony was and what Mandy would shortly be doing with him.

"That was the end of it," the Governor said. He was no longer telling me, he was talking to himself. "I had just paid off one scumbag and she was hopping into bed with another. Pretty soon I would have to deal with a whole succession of blackmailers."

Maxie's fatal mistake was reading the murder in Alfred O'Hare's eyes. Probably it was a look he was already familiar with, considering his background and his ready offer to take Mandy out of the picture.

"That was how he said it," said the Governor. "'I'll take her out of the picture, gramps.' And then he laughed. He thought he was being funny, equating that with the snapshots. And I laughed along with him. But it was something else I thought was funny. That scum wasn't going to live much longer, and *that* was very funny indeed."

Jon Maxfield must have been blinded by visions of easy gold. Finding out that Mandy was from money and that her father was in politics had been like finding one nugget in a creek bed. It was good for a few thousand, but unless he found another nugget, that would be the end of it. And then Alfred O'Hare was ready for murder and a whole mountain of gold opened before him. For a certain sum he would arrange the death of the granddaughter, with

Tony as a perfect fall guy. And then he could continue the extortion day after day, month after month, with the old man caught in his web. He seemed to be the perfect victim. Elderly, wealthy, and willing to pay anything to buy himself political immortality through the vehicle of his only son.

Perfect. Or not quite perfect. Because the elderly gentleman had waited in that fetid alley and when Maxfield came out to dispose of the knife that murdered Mandy it had ended up deep between his shoulder blades.

"See this here?" said the Governor, meeting my eyes again as he indicated the prone figure between us. "Believe it or not it was still asleep when I went in to leave the knife on the floor. Snoring away with his mouth open and my slut of a granddaughter dead beside him. It was pitiable and comic. Rather like one of those Hogarth etchings, updated to the twentieth century."

I decided to try nodding again. He had the gun, so nodding made sense. The other thing that made sense was what Alfred O'Hare was telling me. Hiring Maxfield to kill Mandy was on "impulse," because of his "temper," but what happened after that had a certain cold logic to it.

Seeing me at the funeral gave him the idea of retaining my services. Killing two birds, was how he put it, the first being the possibility that I might decide to nose around on my own, the second being that I would deliver information regarding the police investigation, information that a man like Stein might not willingly relinquish directly to Alfred O'Hare. Oh, I had been a handy dandy detective. Well worth the per diem simply for calling to tell him that Tony Steel had been sprung.

"I assumed that birds flock together," said the Governor with an air of satisfaction. "Dirty little birds. The homo friend of Gerald's was already putting feelers out, trying to shake me down. I was biding my time, waiting for this thing here to make bail. I knew he would come to be very useful. . . ."

That had been Randy's fatal mistake. Calling the old man to tell him he had seen a certain Mercedes sedan in the parking lot of the Play Pen the night Mandy was murdered, a vision of incongruous luxury he was willing to forget for a certain sum. Truman Hawkins's fatal mistake was in being at the beach cottage to interview the two strippers when the Governor came to call.

"He was a brave little man," said Alfred O'Hare. He finished the Scotch and tossed the glass away. It was good crystal and it broke musically. "I think he thought he had saved your life at the price of his own. All that nervous nonsense over the telephone, remember? When all I wanted was a witness who would testify that this little bailed-out wop had shot his faggot friend and an over-ambitious, small-time reporter. No, dear, I wasn't planning to include you in the scenario. But then you went and found out about Byron. Which is a pity, because Byron's accident didn't have anything to do with this. And I must say your disloyalty to Mandy was rather shocking. As if *she* knew what happened down by the pond, or cared enough about Pudge to want to ruin things for him. Shocking! I do believe my first intuition was correct. You were jealous of the little slut because she took your playboy husband to bed."

I forgot about only nodding and shook my head vigorously. That made the Governor laugh. He laughed and laughed. I couldn't see my watch because my hands were bound up behind me; he may have laughed for a minute or more, long enough to chill my blood. For some reason it was worse hearing him laugh than hearing him tell me how he was going to make things look. How Tony Steel had abducted me and driven up to "Serenity" to demand that the Governor pay ransom for his private investigator and how the Governor of course had been more than willing to do that but Tony, being a nervous brand of guinea, shot me anyway and how that elderly but virile public hero, Alfred

194

O'Hare, Sr., had struggled for the gun and killed the ethnic roughneck while receiving a painful but relatively safe flesh wound.

"Right here," he said, indicating his left bicep. "Right through the meat of the muscle. Oh, I'm sure it will hurt. That's why I'm dosing myself with Scotch. I dislike physical pain, you know. I find it demeaning. But my being wounded will give the scene a touch of realism, don't you agree? They'll have to believe me."

The dancer, who had been taking all of this in with increasing agitation, began to flail about. I could see his arms straining, the cords on his wrists standing out. His head was shaking from side to side and he was biting at the gag. I think he had something to say and he knew the time to say it was growing short. His eyes had lost their fear.

That was his fatal mistake, because the Governor leaned over, put the pistol in his left eye, and pulled the trigger. That was when the steel door flew open and Pudge came in at a run.

"Oh Jesus!" he said. "Oh God in heaven!"

I think he'd been listening at the door. I think he had been planning to burst in eventually and the gunshot had come as a surprise. He looked down at the shattered head of his daughter's last lover and he wept.

The Governor was taking it all calmly. He put a consoling arm around his son and he looked surprised when Pudge shrugged him off.

"I did it for you, boy," he said.

Pudge asked him for the gun.

"Maybe this is for the good of us," said his father. "Maybe this happened so you can help me. This is your test of fire, boy. This is what makes you a man."

I had to give him credit. He was still in there plugging for himself. And it may have been that he actually believed that Pudge would help him dispose of me and arrange the bodies into a suitable scenario.

"Give me the gun," said Pudge.

He gave him the gun. Pudge raised it and shot him through the heart. The old man had the courtesy not to look surprised or hurt. He kept standing, however, until Pudge emptied the gun into his chest, at which point he collapsed forward, into his son's arms.

They both slumped down. Pudge looked pale and serene. He cradled the old man's great white head and spoke to him as the light faded from his lizard eyes.

"I believed you," he said. "When you fought with Byron I believed you when you said you fought for my honor. I didn't think it was right that you killed him, but I thought *you* thought it was right. You standing there up to your knees in the muck of that pond and Byron floating there dead and you telling me it was because he had screwed my wife. And it was true, wasn't it? It was true, but I didn't understand *how* it was true until Elisha told me. She waited thirty years to tell me. To tell me that *you* had been screwing her for most of the summer and when your big brother got wind of it he thought he'd try a little piece for himself. The both of you getting the poor girl drunk. And when you found out that Uncle Byron had been getting what you took for your very own you came storming down that path and the two of you rolled in the grass like a couple of lovesick boys, only you were mad enough to kill and he wasn't. But killing your own brother wasn't bad enough. You had to convince me that it was *my* fault. All these years."

He had his hands entwined in the old man's head and he was making it shake and nod as he talked, as if the body was a big, loose, ventriloquist's dummy.

"Did you know that 'Lisha talks to all of us? Byron and Louise and Alfie and now Mandy and you and me? She talks to all of us."

I knew then, watching the son cradle his father's head in his lap, that insanity can be passed like a torch, or a hot bullet, each to each.

196

Pudge picked up the gun and put it in his mouth and pulled the trigger. When he lost interest in clicking away at empty chambers he finally noticed me. I had rolled over and was butting my knees against him.

He put the empty pistol in his suitcoat pocket and proceeded to untie me.

"Father was an Eagle Scout," he told me solemnly. "That's where he learned to tie good knots."

The siren had been coming up the mountain for a while. I took Pudge by the hand and walked him out of the concrete room. We went up the stairwell and outside, into the morning. In the daylight Byron's last construction was wet, gleaming, and ugly. Down in the valley a gray snake of fog still clung to the creek bed.

Sheriff Krankow got out of his cruiser, holding a pistol at his side, pointed downward. Richard came out of the passenger side, looking worried and happy. Dr. Sutcliffe got out of the rear door, holding his black grip. Pudge looked through them, his gentle eyes gone distant.

"I'm going to ask Elisha if I can move into her room," he told me. "We can all be together again."

I told him it sounded like a fine idea. And then I asked him to tell Mandy I forgave her. I really meant it, finally.

www.ingramcontent.com/pod-product-compliance
Lightning Source LLC
Chambersburg PA
CBHW020601250626
47154CB00004B/1315